Best *of* Enemies

SUZANNE PIERSON
ELLISON

rising moon

Books for Young Readers from Northland Publishing

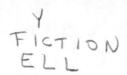

Y
FICTION
ELL

This book is dedicated to My Precious Turquoise.

The text type was set in Adobe Caslon
The display type was set in Celestia Antiqua
Roadrunner Icon set in Artifact
Composed and manufactured in the United States of America
Designed by Sandy Bell
Edited by Stephanie Bucholz
Production Supervised by Lisa Brownfield

FIRST IMPRESSION
ISBN 0-87358-714-6 (hc)
ISBN 0-87358-717-0 (sc)

Library of Congress Catalog Card Number 98-25547

Ellison, Suzanne Pierson, 1951–
Best of Enemies / Suzanne Pierson Ellison.
201 p. cm.
Summary: Three young people from very different backgrounds—the
son of a wealthy New Mexican rancher, a Navajo slave, and a young Texan
soldier—who find themselves held for ransom by a pair of horse thieves
learn to look beyond their differences.
ISBN 0-87358-714-6 (hc.). — ISBN 0-87358-717-0 (sc.)
[1. New Mexico—History—Civil War, 1861–1865—Juvenile fiction.
2. New Mexico—History—Civil War, 1861–1865—Fiction. 3.
Friendship—Fiction.] I. Title.
PZ7.E47655Be 1998
[Fic]—dc21   3. Historical fiction   98-25547

699/2M/9-98 (hc)
699/3.5M/9-98 (sc)

A NOTE FROM THE AUTHOR

The main characters in *Best of Enemies* are fictional, but each represents a genuine point of view held in the mid-1900s by his or her group of people.

Most history books cite slavery as the cause of the American Civil War, but soldiers volunteered for many reasons. Some wanted glory or adventure. Northerners promised to preserve the Union. Southerners vowed to save their homes. Both sides claimed they fought for freedom.

Most of the battles took place in the South. This meant that the Southerners, or Confederates, were fighting to protect their land from the invading Northerners, also called Yankees.

Only in New Mexico did a prolonged battle campaign reverse this situation. When Texans, under Confederate command, marched up the Rio Grande, New Mexicans saw a pattern that had been repeated many times: Texans were coming to steal their land. Many New Mexicans had no loyalty to the U.S. Government, which had seized their territory from Mexico only twenty years before. What mattered to them most was defending their own families.

The Confederates invaded New Mexico for several reasons. First, they wanted the land. Second, they hoped to keep those who opposed slavery from settling close to Texas. Finally, they intended to march from Santa Fe to the goldfields of Colorado and California, where they could also find an outlet to the sea. This was crucial because the U.S. Navy had blockaded most of the harbors in the South. Basic supplies could no longer be shipped to the region, and ordinary people could not buy the things they needed.

When the war broke out, a number of U.S. Army posts on the western frontier were closed so more soldiers could be sent to fight in Virginia, Tennessee, and many other states. As a result, the Indians stepped up their attacks on settlers, hoping to use the war "when the white people fought each other" as an opportunity to reclaim their land and freedom. Local troops and citizens responded by making every effort to crush some tribes completely. They did this by killing warriors, burning food supplies and grazing areas, and capturing women and children.

At one point nearly a third of the Navajo tribe were prisoners of war, not counting those who were forced to live on a reservation. Decades after the Emancipation Proclamation freed all African Americans, Navajos and captives from other tribes continued to be held as slaves in New Mexico. Most of them were never reunited with their people.

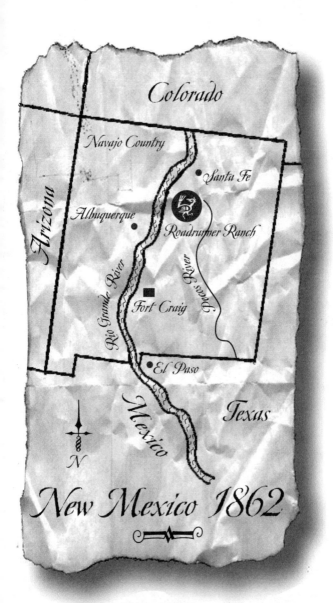

Colorado

Navajo Country

• Santa Fe

Albuquerque •

Roadrunner Ranch

Arizona

Rio Grande River

Pecos River

■ Fort Craig

• El Paso

N

Mexico

Texas

New Mexico 1862

Chapter One

Mundo Rivera liked the way his new spurs jangled as he swaggered across the festively decorated, sunbaked courtyard enclosed by his family's massive adobe house. Nervously he tugged on the gold-piece buttons of his short velvet jacket, then straightened the wide brim of his new black hat. He was used to playing the role of a wealthy landowner's teenage son, but he rarely had to dress the part. In the high desert land of New Mexico, every man, woman, and child was too busy staying alive to waste much time on finery.

Especially when rumor had it that the bloodthirsty Texans were headed up the Rio Grande toward Santa Fe.

There wasn't a living soul in Mundo's valley who hadn't lost a relative the last time Texans had invaded the territory ... or the time before that. For decades, the Texans had been trying to steal parts of New Mexico — including the Riveras' vast and magnificent ranch. Every man in Mundo's family had risked his life at least once to beat back the land-greedy Texans.

If trouble came to Roadrunner Ranch, Mundo vowed to do the same.

But the Riveras had something else to worry about right now besides the enemy. An hour ago, the clatter of hoofbeats had heralded the arrival of the man *Papá* had chosen to marry Mundo's sister, Chayito. Chayito had never met the man. Neither had Mundo, until today.

The wedding date had been pushed up because of the Texas threat, and this afternoon the groom's whole family had arrived to stay with the Riveras for the traditional four-day feast. Roadrunner Ranch was already full of guests and relatives who had traveled—some all the way from Mexico—by horseback, carriage, or on foot. Every rancher, sheepherder, and cowboy in the valley had been invited. Nothing but the imminent threat of battle would keep them away.

"Psssst! Mundo!" a female voice whispered furtively from an iron-barred, open window.

He knew it was his sister, Chayito, who was not allowed to join the guests until after the wedding. She sounded excited and a little breathless, almost scared.

Mundo sauntered slowly toward the window, trying not to give her away. Although he took care not to let people know it, nobody was more important to him than his sister. He knew his father had chosen this match with great concern for the reputation of her bridegroom's family, but Mundo still didn't like the idea of her getting married. Chayito had run the Rivera household for several years, but she was only a year older than Mundo, and sixteen seemed too young to be leaving the brother she still rode with daily.

"Closer!" she insisted.

Mundo nonchalantly turned his back to her and leaned against the thick adobe wall. Nobody could see his sister, but he knew Chayito would be pressed up against the other side.

"Tell me!" she urged, sounding almost desperate. "What does *Don* Victor look like? Is he nice? Does he seem ... kind?"

Mundo wasn't sure how to answer that. He respected his father's judgment, but he couldn't say he'd liked *Don* Victor at first sight. He hoped that was just because his own feelings were getting in the way.

"He looks ... strong. He rides a horse very well. He spoke respectfully to Julio and *Papá*."

Julio was their brother, so much older than Mundo and Chayito that they thought of him almost as an uncle. For as long as Mundo could remember, *Papá* had treated Julio as a man.

At fifteen, Mundo could ride with the skill of a Commanche and hunt when he had to, but his father still treated him like a baby. Knowing what drove *Papá* didn't make it any easier for Mundo to obey him. Sometimes he could barely hide his eagerness for manhood ... or his anger.

The long silence behind him told Mundo that he hadn't said what Chayito wanted to hear.

"Did you see him smile?"

"No."

"Did he . . . ask about me?"

"No."

"Does he act like he knows anything about me at all, or is he just doing what his father orders?"

Keeping his voice low, Mundo answered, "I only met him for a moment, Chayito, and he was talking to Julio, not to me."

"Well, what did he say to Julio?" Chayito pressed.

"He told him that he had another present for you on its way."

"Besides the clothes for me and the stock for *Papá?*"

"Yes."

"What is it?" She sounded a little more hopeful. "Is it . . . something personal?"

"I guess so. It's a Navajo servant. A very fine woolen-blanket weaver. She's still quite young, but *Don* Victor told Julio that she had already learned the trade from the women of her tribe when she was captured a few years ago. By now she's completely tame."

"That's not exactly personal," Chayito replied uneasily. "But I guess at least he's not planning to work me to death."

There wasn't much Mundo could say to that. The Riveras had owned Navajos before. They were treacherous. Captivity did not usually make them gentle. Still, it was customary in the Riveras' social class to give a Navajo captive to a bride to help with the work. Mundo had to admit that nobody could make blankets like a properly trained Navajo weaver. From *Don* Victor's point of view, it was a gracious gift.

"*Don* Victor said one of the wagons broke down, the one the Navajo was riding in," Mundo mentioned. "He left two men to fix it and come along when they could. They should be all right if they get here before the sun sets."

"Surely *Papá* will send someone to help. If the Navajo warriors know that only two men are guarding the servant, it would be a perfect time to stage a raid. Doesn't *Don* Victor know—"

"I don't think it was his decision," Mundo interjected. *Don* Victor was about thirty years old, but Mundo guessed his father made all the major decisions for the family. His employees all called the old man *El Patrón*, "the boss."

"Probably not," Chayito agreed. She sounded too soft, too uncertain for his normally spunky sister. "Didn't he say anything else about the wedding?"

Mundo sighed. He would not lie to his sister, and it troubled him that he could do nothing to ease her worries.

"None of the men talked about it much. They all wanted to know the latest news about the Texans. They seem to be getting closer. *Don* Victor told Julio that he'd heard that three thousand soldiers have crossed the border at El Paso and are heading north to Fort Craig."

Chayito took a deep breath. "Do they think there will be war before the wedding?"

Mundo thought she already knew the answer. She just didn't want to think about it.

"There's already been shooting near the fort, but Julio says it's only skirmishing between the scouts and pickets." He didn't remind her that the wedding date had already been moved up a month to be sure the priest could complete the ceremony before there was any local trouble with the Texans. If by some unlikely chance the invaders managed to squeak past the U.S. regulars and the New Mexican Militia, every man in the valley would fight to the death before he gave up a single grain of sand.

Before Chayito could ask him anything else, Mundo heard the thud of fresh hoofbeats, usually followed by the cheerful greetings of the assembled visitors as they welcomed the arriving wedding guests.

But there were no greetings this time, no sounds of welcome, no happy notes of joy. Suddenly the huge courtyard grew completely silent.

Mundo left Chayito without a word and crossed through the visitors to join his father and brother at the massive gates that today stood open to the windy grassland. Past the paloverdes that circled the compound, he could see a group of riders thundering toward him. They leaned forward in their saddles, pressing hard. The two lead horses were lathered white with sweat.

The crowd in the courtyard held perfectly still, as though holding one great communal breath. Nobody said a word until the horses galloped inside the protection of the thick adobe walls.

"The Texans are coming!" the first rider shouted as he pulled up his mount. "They broke through our lines at Fort Craig! We need every man!"

Chapter Two

"We ain't gonna make the Roadrunner 'fore dark," warned the cowboy in the sheepskin chaps.

He was talking to the carrot-haired man who shared the driver's seat of *El Patrón*'s oldest wagon. Hours had passed since either one had spoken to the Navajo girl dressed in a faded yellow skirt, a pink sash, and a frayed black *rebozo* wrapped around her head and shoulders. Tenchi rode in the wagon bed squished between a dozen bags of flour, a stack of lumber, and three piles of fine woolen blankets she had woven.

"If *Don* Victor wasn't so all-fired up over his wedding, he wouldn't have left us out here alone with that Navajo," Carrot-Top complained as dusk purpled the ragged land.

"Asking for the Injuns to come after us, I'd say," agreed Sheepskin Chaps. "Ain't a soul in a hundred miles don't know how much stock *El Patrón* drove to the Roadrunner today for the wedding."

It wasn't the first time Tenchi had heard him point out that fact. They had started out from *El Patrón*'s great ranch in a neighboring valley with half a dozen wagons, a host of riders, and a herd of cattle and fine Spanish horses. But around midday, Tenchi's wagon had hit a rough patch of ground and split an axle. Assigned to fix the break and follow on their own, the two cowboys had been left behind.

El Patrón's men had griped the whole time they worked on the repairs, keeping half an eye on Tenchi. She'd sat alone in a clump of blue grama grass, unable to find protection from the endless dust devils that pummeled her all day. Topsoil wind was common in this dry country, and was much worse during a drought. As much as Tenchi longed for the stinging wind to stop, she longed for rain.

But she was used to longing for things she could not have—food, friends, freedom—and she did not complain. She had given up complaining long ago.

"Gonna have to find somewhere to camp," Sheepskin Chaps whined. "Ain't a lick of shelter for miles. Least ways, not that I can see."

Tenchi knew that in her other life she would have known how to find shelter anywhere. To Navajos, the land was a home, a friend, a weapon. But it had been years since she had spoken Navajo or left the safety of Santa Fe. She no longer knew how to be an Indian.

She had been kidnapped at the age of eight by a band of unsavory traders who caught and sold Navajos for a living. Since most of the people of New Mexico— Yankees, Hispanics, and several other Indian tribes—

were usually at war with the Navajos, the hunters were praised for killing warriors and bringing in women and children. The captives gave New Mexicans free labor and helped break down the tribe.

Tenchi had been caught with a dozen of her people, including her aunt and some of her cousins. At first they vowed to escape, and several of them tried. One was shot down before her eyes. Another disappeared. Tenchi herself was caught and beaten three times.

One by one the other captives from her tribe and family were sold to different places, until Tenchi ended up alone. There was no one to share her sorrow, her language, or her old way of life. In eight years she had lived with five different owners, both Hispanic and Yankee, some cold and ruthless, some a little more kind. She was now nearly seventeen, the age when girls from her tribe took a husband and moved to a hogan near their mothers'. As a little girl, this had been her greatest dream. But now she never expected to have a friend or sister or brother again, let alone children of her own.

"You heard much about Navajo trouble lately?" the carrot-haired man asked in a lowered voice.

"There's always Navajo trouble," Sheepskin Chaps muttered grimly. "And from what we heard in town, it don't sound like the Texans are too far away."

There was a tense silence in the wagon as it rumbled and bounced along. Nobody needed to mention the other dangers that lurked on the desert at night: rattlers and coral snakes, packs of wolves, rustlers of every hue. As for the Navajos ...

There had been a time when Tenchi had spent every

day waiting for the warriors of her tribe to come to rescue her, and every night sobbing because they had not. She did not know if they had forgotten her, lost track of where she'd been sold, or were themselves all murdered. She did not even know if she would be able to remember enough of her language to make it clear to the warriors that she wanted to go with them. She was excited at the prospect of a daring Navajo rescue but, to her shame, she was also afraid.

Still, the possibility of a nighttime raid caused a little sunflower of hope to grow in her heart, a sunny yellow blossom that she thought had long since shriveled and died. Long ago, she had learned that escape was impossible in crowded Santa Fe. But out here in the wilderness, with only two Yankee cowboys between herself and freedom . . .

Before Tenchi could finish the thought, Sheepskin Chaps seemed to read her mind.

"Once we stop and get a fire goin', Navajo, me and Carrot-Top is gonna shake out our bedrolls and chain you to a wheel," he barked. "So don't you be gettin' no funny notions 'bout slittin' our throats and slitherin' off tonight."

"We must defend our land!" roared one of the wedding guests. "We must all ride out at dawn!"

His proclamation brought a round of huzzahs from the men gathered in the Riveras' grand salon. It was the first time Mundo had ever been present at such a meeting, which always excluded women and children. He hung back, almost out of sight behind a massive chair, hoping his father would not order him away.

"Of course we must send men to the battle!" one of Mundo's uncles agreed. "But what about our families? If we all go, they will have no protection. We can't send them home alone without an escort!"

At once the other guests began to voice their opinions. Some thought each man should defend his own home. Others thought that everyone should ride to the Yankee stronghold at Fort Union or catch up with the volunteer militia as the troops moved along the Rio Grande. Some thought that the women and children and old people who had came to the wedding should remain at Roadrunner Ranch with a small group of men to protect them.

Julio assured everyone that the Roadrunner should be considered home to their families as long as necessary. But *Papá* did not speak right away. Mundo knew he was worried about the reputation of his family as well as his daughter's future. Once a wedding was canceled, for any reason, it was hard to get offers of marriage for a girl again. Besides, it was unthinkable to start a wedding festival, invite all the friends and relatives, lodge the priest, then cancel everything without even notifying the other guests who were still on the way! But neither was it possible to refuse the call to arms of one's country when it was being overrun by Texans ... no matter how long it might take them to actually reach Santa Fe.

"I mean no disrespect to you or your daughter," *El Patrón* said firmly, "but we have no choice."

He was a big man compared to Mundo's father, broad across the shoulders and solid beneath his belt. His hair was still black and thick, not scraggly gray like *Papá*'s.

"Our men must leave at daybreak," he commanded. "The wedding will have to wait."

Papá looked chagrined.

Before he could speak, *Don* Victor offered another suggestion. "Perhaps ... since it is wartime ... we could have the priest complete the mass tonight, so there would be no question of our contractual arrangement."

"My sister deserves a real wedding!" Mundo burst out. "If you cannot wait to do it right—"

"I'm sure *Don* Victor meant no offense," Julio interrupted briskly, his warning glance ordering his little brother to silence. "He is merely helping us to consider alternatives."

Mundo knew he should not have spoken, but his need to protect his sister suddenly swelled within him, not just because of the wedding but because of the war.

"There are no alternatives," *Papá* said grimly. "We thought we had more time."

Nobody answered. Mundo knew they were all thinking the same thing: they had believed that the Texans would be stopped completely at Fort Craig. Instead they had overrun the regular U.S. Army forces and scattered the New Mexican volunteers. Pride was no longer a great enough reason to pretend their homes and families were not in danger.

"I regret the outcome of our arrangement," *El Patrón* respectfully said to *Papá*. "When we are free to celebrate, we can discuss this union once again."

Papá's face flushed. *El Patrón* wasn't exactly backing off, but he was hinting that if the Riveras lost everything to the Texans, the wedding might no longer be in *Don* Victor's best interest.

Stiffly, Julio said, "We can discuss the wedding later. We need to prepare for the Texans now."

As the men marched off to find their wives and children, Mundo found himself alone with Julio and his father. It seemed too quiet in the grand, empty room, still festively decorated for the wedding. None of the Riveras spoke until the servant who came in to stoke the fire had left discreetly.

"*Papá*, one of us must stay here to supervise. It is our home, our responsibility—"

"I know." *Papá*'s voice was dark.

"You are the *señor* of the Roadrunner Ranch," Julio continued with deference. "Perhaps it would be better if you were to stay and I—"

"No!" *Papá* practically hollered. "I will not hide with women and children while the Texans threaten my land! I will not give them another son!"

He had said it now, released the raging tide of grief that Mundo knew he always carried with him. Once before he had tried to do what was right, to protect his family single-handedly while marauding Texans had overrun the ranch. There had been six Rivera children then, and Julio had not been the oldest son.

"*Papá*, letting the Texans kill you won't bring any of them back." Julio didn't say "my brothers."

But their names hung in the air. Mundo had been a newborn when the Texans came, and he did not remember his brothers' faces. He knew that there had been three others—*Papá*'s firstborn and two between Julio and Chayito—and the Texans had slaughtered them all. *Mamá* had managed to hide her two babies, Chayito and Mundo, under an old saddle in the horse barn. Then the Texans killed her, too.

They left *Papá* bullet-holed and bleeding, with eight-year-old Julio sobbing in his arms.

"I know I can't bring them back. But I can keep *you* alive!" *Papá*'s face was growing red. "And maybe I can kill some of them before they spill my blood on New Mexican soil."

"*Papá*, you shouldn't go alone," Julio insisted. "I always thought we'd go to war together. But with all these people counting on us, somebody has to stay here. And if—"

"*I will go to war!*" *Papá* shouted. "I will make the Texans pay for what they have done to me, even if I fight them all by myself!"

In the heavy silence that followed, Mundo dared to murmur, "You don't have to stay here, *Papá*, and you don't have to go alone." His voice began to squeak, as it often did at awkward moments. "You have another son."

Papá turned to stare at him. So did Julio. It was obvious to Mundo that neither of them had even considered the possibility that he would join them.

"You are a child. I would never let you risk your life in such a foolish manner. Besides, you are not very skilled with a gun."

Mundo felt a surge of anger. He could shoot well enough. And nobody could outride him!

He had made his offer as a man. *Papá* had no right to sweep him aside.

"You are not the only one who lost something to the Texans!" he answered in a tone of voice that he never used with *Papá*. "You are not the only member of this family who wants revenge!"

This time it was Julio who turned on him. "Chayito needs you. She has no mother, and maybe no husband, either, after this war is over. If anything happens to *Papá*—"

"Then she will have *you*," Mundo answered grimly. He knew that Julio was right—nobody was closer to Chayito than he was—but he also knew that his family would treat him like a child forever until he stood up and proved himself as a man. "Besides, what will she have if we lose our land to the Texans?" he demanded. "Do you want them to trample the Roadrunner again?"

"Mundo!" *Papá* shouted. "Don't you *ever* say—"

He froze—they all froze—as they heard a man clear his throat just outside the door.

It was *El Patrón*. "I am sorry to intrude," he declared, not sounding sorry at all. "But I wanted to ask you if you might loan us a guide who knows the land to go see if we can find our missing wagon. In all the confusion, we did not realize that it had not arrived by sundown."

It was a reasonable request. Except for the piney-oak uplands to the north and east of Rivera land, the Road-runner was a mass of half-dry prairie grasses, peppered here and there with cactus, ravines, and outcrops of sharp rocks. Only somebody who'd cowboyed there for years would be able to find his way around in the dark.

"I will go," Julio volunteered promptly. "Most of the men will be riding out with you tomorrow and should rest all they can tonight."

El Patrón nodded his thanks in a dignified manner, then bid goodnight to *Papá*. He took a few steps from the room, with Julio right behind him, before he stopped and turned to glance at Mundo.

Then he did something a guest would never do in a New Mexican house outside of wartime.

"This is no time to be selfish," he criticized *Papá*. "Let the boy come."

Papá flushed, mouth agape, too shocked at first to answer.

Julio lifted a hand, as though to silence *El Patrón*, but the rich old man pressed on.

"You are not the only man in New Mexico who has lost someone to the Texans," he said bitterly, "and you are not the only one who must banish them with the price of a son."

Chapter Three

Sheepskin Chaps meant what he said. He threw Tenchi a blue-and-red blanket—one a former owner had allowed her to keep—and chained her to the wagon wheel just after dark. It was a long time since she'd been tied up—since her first year of captivity, in fact—and the humiliation was hard to bear.

So was the cold. When the sun went down, even in the summer, the heat vanished. This time of year, the dust-bearing winds were frigid, and sometimes, there was snow.

There was no snow tonight, but the winds were slashing at the sideoats and needlegrass ... and at Tenchi.

I wonder how I could have imagined an escape tonight? she asked herself glumly. Even if there was a Navajo raiding party out, the warriors were too smart to risk their lives for two horses, fine blankets, and some flour. And they would carry no tool that could cut through her chains.

Still, she waited, too tense and cold to sleep. She thought of all the blankets she had woven since her capture—and the ones she had woven with her aunt and mother before that—and wondered why she could not snuggle up under more than one of them now. She loved weaving, because she was so skilled at it, and because it was a gift from a dozen generations of the women of her family. But she hated it, too, because it was the price of her bondage, a piece of herself that her owners bought and sold without even knowing they were gouging out part of her Navajo soul.

The cowboys lay by the fire snoring loudly. Tenchi wasn't sure whether they had denied her its soothing heat out of cruelty, fear, or simple ignorance. It probably did not occur to them that she was human, that she needed warmth and shelter as much as anyone.

The wind picked up and the temperature dropped a few degrees. The soil-laden air battered Tenchi's face without mercy. Behind her came the hooting of a great horned owl, reminding her of the nighttime ghosts that always threatened Navajos. She could hear the rustling of little creatures in the grass, but she could not tell what sort of animals they might be.

And then, with no warning, one of them snorted.

It was a horse.

But the cowboys had only two horses, the wagon's draft team, and both were hobbled on the far side of the fire. Tenchi could make out their silhouettes in the occasional sparks and flames.

Still, there was a horse behind her.

It could have been a stray from a winter remuda. It could have been part of a nearby rancher's herd. It could even have been the mount of some lonely traveler. But anyone could clearly see the cowboys sleeping by the fire. An innocent man would have greeted them.

Tenchi heard the sound of hooves shuffling toward her now. She could tell that there was at least one other horse. Both beasts were moving closer.

It had been years since she had been kidnapped, but she had not lost *all* the skills she had been given by her people. She knew that trouble was coming. If she had crouched near any friend or family, she would have shouted out a warning.

She would have taken steps to escape and survive.

But she felt no allegiance to the cowboys. She did not even hold the cautious affection she had once felt for one owner's wife or a later one's children. *El Patrón*'s men had not abused her, but they had shown her no kindness, either. In the morning they would pass her on to another owner, a thoughtless young bride who would, no doubt, order her to weave until her fingers were stiff and swollen, or sell her, in time, to yet another stranger who would command the same.

These fleeting thoughts, however, were overrun by another, more compelling notion. *The horses could be mounts of Navajos.* There had been a time when Tenchi dreamed of nothing but her freedom, when she still dreamed at all. For an instant, she saw a vision of her father and uncles coming to rescue her. Then she realized that, even if these raiders were blood kin, she would no longer recognize them.

A second later it came to her that the raiders could not be warriors from her tribe. She had heard them, heard them clearly. No Navajo would have brought his horses close enough to make a sound! Whoever was out there was someone else, someone who might be as great a threat to Tenchi as to the sleeping men. Silently she pressed herself against the iron-rimmed wheel, hoping the intruders would have no reason to glance at the wagon.

"I only see two," she heard a man whisper. A Texan, by his drawl.

Another Texan said, "I'll take out the one on the right."

An instant later, gunshots roared out of the silence. Tenchi stifled a scream. Sheepskin Chaps jerked upright for just an instant, reaching for his gun, but he could not fire it before he was shot down.

Carrot-Top never even woke up.

"I heard a girl cry out," yelled one of the shooters. "Find her while I locate the rest of the stock. There should be a small herd somewhere."

Tenchi heard one horse trot off. She gazed at the dead men by the fire, suddenly feeling great kindness toward them, and guilt that she had not tried to save them.

But that moment of sympathy was lost in her own terror. The outlaws would kill her the instant they found her by the wagon. She knew that, bound by her chains, she could not crawl underneath it; she'd already tried that seeking shelter. Any attempt to creep off would announce her presence as the chains jangled and grew taut. She had no weapons. She could cower until they found her, or . . . think of something else.

The killers were Texans. She knew that Texans hated New Mexicans almost as much as New Mexicans hated them. Navajos hated New Mexicans, too. More than once her people had joined with another tribe of uncertain allegiance to go on the warpath against a mutual enemy. Maybe if she told these men she was Navajo . . .

Quickly she dismissed the idea. To most frontier rustlers, one Indian was the same as another. Being a Navajo would probably not count in her favor.

She pushed aside her panic. *I need to think like a rich man,* Tenchi told herself. She had learned a lot from her owners, most of whom had lived for money. They didn't care whether their stock-in-trade was a horse or a gold mine or a human; if there was a way to earn a profit, they were always willing to make a trade. *If I can find a way to dangle cash before their eyes . . .*

"Hello! I'm over here!" she called out as she struggled with a sudden notion. "Those horrible Yankees chained me to the wagon!"

At first there was no answer. Then a gruff Texan voice ordered, "Stand up where I can see you. Hands way out."

Slowly Tenchi rose to her feet. It was not easy after leaning against the wooden spokes for so many hours. "I'm trying," she called out, forcing her voice to sound grateful and friendly. She spoke English and Spanish fluently, but she still carried the accent of her native tongue. "I can only put up one hand. The other is flat to the wheel."

She heard the horse step closer. By the moonlight, she could see the man on its back.

He was in his twenties, bearded, with a hard-looking, small mouth. His front teeth were rotted. One was missing. His face showed no expression, but Tenchi knew she had taken him off guard. It was one thing to kill an enemy, another to gun down a female stranger who claims to think you've come charging in to rescue her.

"What're you doin' out here?" he asked suspiciously.

"I was captured by those Yankees. You know ... you know how they are."

He grunted in agreement. Still, he kept his revolver pointed in her direction. At least he did not shoot.

"You ain't no Texas gal. And you don't sound like no Mexican or Injun, neither."

Tenchi struggled to think of a way to save herself. "I'm a ... Santa Fe servant from a local tribe," she admitted, trying to emphasize her usefulness. "I was captured when I was quite young, but I'm a very skilled weaver. I'm worth a lot of money to a merchant or a rancher."

He did not reply at once. Tenchi held her breath. She expected no mercy from an outlaw, but she knew she'd offered him the one thing he would want.

At last he said, "We wasn't thinkin' along the lines of Injuns or slaves. Kurtzer says we was just lookin' for horses."

There was an awkward pause. The longer he waited to kill her, Tenchi was certain, the harder it would be for him to do.

The wind rose again. Tenchi let the silence wear thin.

"Lookee here, I don't know about this," the young man finally conceded. "When Kurtzer gets back—"

"Tell him you can sell me for the price of a half dozen Spanish horses."

Morning came, it seemed to Mundo, before he had even shut his eyes.

It had been a long, unsettling night. Julio had led some of *El Patrón*'s men out to the place where they'd left the wagon, but they could find no sign of it, or the men either, in the dark. Over and over again they'd combed the waving grama grass from the spot where the axle had broken to the main gates of the ranch. They'd searched for any possible site for a night camp in between. By dawn, *El Patrón* was insisting that he "owed it to his men" to stay at the Roadrunner until he found out what had happened and, if necessary, stage some sort of a rescue.

Mundo told Julio, once they were alone, that he thought *El Patrón* just didn't want to go fight the Texans.

"Are you sure *you* do?" Julio had replied. "Sometimes, we say things when we feel proud and angry that . . . later we wish we could take back."

Mundo had already had time to be sorry he'd spoken so sharply to his father, but he was more determined than ever to prove he was a man. Besides, Julio was staying at the ranch, and it would not be right to let *Papá* go into battle without one of his sons.

Even if it was the one who'd broken the rules and talked back to him.

Mundo mounted his chestnut mare as the darkness began to ease. Chayito, wrapped in a heavy shawl, furtively slipped out to wish him godspeed.

"You will come back alive!" she ordered. "I mean it, Mundo. I'll never forgive you if you die."

The words made no sense, but Mundo understood. His sister squeezed the toe of his shoe so hard it hurt, then wiped half-hidden tears as she said goodbye.

Julio's farewell was more grave. He did something he had never done before—he shook Mundo's hand.

Mundo swallowed hard and stared at his big brother. He had always respected Julio but never really felt close to him. It was something he suddenly wished he could change.

"You take care of yourself, and I will take care of Chayito," Julio promised. His proud voice seemed to tremble. "But *Papá* is too hot with revenge right now to be prudent. Watch him closely, Mundo. You may hold his life in your hands."

Chapter Four

It was bitterly cold at daybreak. The air was awash with swirling sand. Mundo, determined to show no weakness in front of his father, tried to pretend he didn't mind. The Roadrunner cowboys pulled their bandannas over their mouths and noses, but they made no comment. All that mattered to them was how fast they could reach the Texans.

Carrying Roadrunner supplies for the Yankees and herding extra horses, they headed straight across the valley, southwest toward Albuquerque. It was the next town of any real size between Fort Craig and Santa Fe. The Texans would not only try to seize the weapons and ammunition stored there, but would surely loot and forage from the local homes and ranches. They could not have brought enough supplies with them across the desert. Like a flock of locusts, they would seize, eat, or destroy everything in their way.

None of the cowboys said much as they traveled. Normally they laughed and joked among themselves and sometimes, carefully, teased Mundo, always aware that he was their wealthy owner's younger son. But today they were grave. The ranch foreman slipped him some extra jerky and tossed him a canteen around mid-morning, even though Mundo already had one. He ordered the other cowboys to stretch out then, some far in front of Mundo, and always some behind, and Mundo had the feeling that they weren't just riding that way to be ready for the Texans. They were protecting *him*.

The knowledge gave him comfort, and it embarrassed him. He had not come along as a spectator. Even though his riding clothes marked him as an aristocrat, he had come to fight the enemy, to defend his people, to protect his land.

He had come to prove he was a man.

But he wasn't one, that much was certain, in the eyes of his father. Mundo had stayed close to *Papá*, who hardly seemed to notice that his younger son had ridden off to war with him. He did not stop for food or water. He did not speak to anyone. Ever since *El Patrón* had overruled his authority in *Papá*'s own house—and hinted at canceling the wedding—he hadn't seemed like Mundo's proud father. But Mundo knew that the change had more to do with the Texans than with *El Patrón*.

Once or twice, Mundo tried to break the awful silence.

"Do you think we'll be able to stop the Texans before they reach Santa Fe?"

Papá did not even look at him.

"Do you think *Don* Victor will still want to marry Chayito after all this is over?"

Papá gave no hint that he'd heard.

"*Papá*, do you even know I'm here?" Mundo finally begged.

Only then did *Papá* turn to him, his black eyes grave.

"I know you should *not* be here," he answered darkly. "You must hide somewhere when the shooting starts."

Mundo had several hours to ponder *Papá*'s grim comments before he heard another rider lope up behind him. He glanced back nonchalantly, expecting to see a Roadrunner cowboy, or maybe the old foreman. To Mundo's surprise, he spotted *Don* Victor.

Don Victor was a tall, slim man, handsome in a somber sort of way. As usual, he was not smiling. But neither did he look as cold and indifferent to Mundo as he had seemed yesterday.

He tipped his broad-brimmed hat ever so slightly in greeting. Mundo nodded back, but said nothing. They rode on in silence for several moments before *Don* Victor started speaking.

"It took a lot of courage, Mundo, for you to volunteer to fight the Texans," he said as though the two of them chatted every day.

Mundo was surprised . . . and embarrassed. He wasn't feeling particularly courageous today. "No more than it took you, or any of the rest of them," he protested.

Don Victor shook his head. "No, what you did was special. *I* had no choice. The cowboys had nothing much to lose. But you—you have everything to live for." He gave Mundo a half-sad little smile. "Besides, you had to face up to your *papá*, even to cross him. Believe me, I know how hard that is to do."

Mundo knew that *Don* Victor followed the old way, just as Julio did. Respect for a man's elders always came first.

"I guess you would have lost face with *El Patrón*, and the men, if you had stayed behind," Mundo offered.

Don Victor tried to laugh. "I would have lost *everything*," he countered. "I am only in line to inherit my father's holdings because my older brother displeased him. He would cut me off in a second if I did the same." After an awkward pause, he added, "And it would break his crusty old heart completely."

Mundo wasn't sure what to say to that. He glanced around him, trying to look brave and wary. For some time now they had been plodding under the shadow of the mountains, and now the horses were starting to slip over fallen branches and half-crushed pine cones. Piles of rocks lay everywhere, as though they'd been tossed around by an earthquake or a giant having a tantrum.

"Mundo, there is something else I've been wanting to say to you," *Don* Victor continued. He waited until Mundo reluctantly met his eyes. "When I offered to quickly marry your sister before we left for battle, I meant no offense—not to you, not to your family, and certainly not to Chayito." There was another awkward pause. "I was trying to protect her."

"From what?" Mundo blurted out. Before he'd learned that the Texans had won the day at Fort Craig, the only thing he'd thought his sister needed protection from was marriage.

Don Victor brushed back one side, then the other, of his long mustache. "There is a reason my father is known as *El Patrón*," he said quietly. "When I was little, I thought it was his real name. I felt as though I was just one of his Indian servants."

Mundo glanced away. It was growing colder, but the trees cut the worst of the wind.

"He is the 'boss,' in every way. No man dares to cross him. My mother never even raises her voice when he's home."

A silence, strained but sympathetic, fell between them.

"I'm telling you this only so you will understand, so you can make your sister understand—" his voice grew low, "if I do not make it back to tell her myself."

Mundo was astonished. It was the first time *Don* Victor had even hinted that he knew Chayito was a real person.

"I have not met your sister, but I have . . . watched her from a distance for a very long time. I wanted to marry her before I left so she would be protected. Once she is my wife, my father will be honor bound to take care of her always. Until then, he can cast her aside without the guilt of a more noble man."

At last Mundo understood. He remembered only too well the tone in *El Patrón*'s voice when he had hinted that he would call off the wedding if the Riveras lost too much to the Texans.

"Chayito will be all right," Mundo said proudly,

tossing his chin up just a little. "She is a Rivera, and we Riveras take care of our own. Julio says *Papá* is the richest rancher in our valley."

The look on *Don* Victor's face made him instantly regret his arrogance.

"My father's brother was the richest man in *his* valley until the last time the Texans stormed our land." *Don* Victor's lips grew taut with grief. "They took every head of stock, every grazing acre, and every woman in his family." Gravely he faced Mundo. "They left him with nothing. My father found him dead."

Don Victor's words still lingered in Mundo's mind, echoing his own hidden cowardice and his growing fear for Chayito, when he heard the first shot. It ripped across the twilight silence like the hunting call of a red-tailed hawk. An instant later came the cry of a man who has been mortally wounded and knows he's going to die.

It was one of the Riveras' cowboys.

"Kill the Texans!" screamed the old Roadrunner foreman. "Remember *la señora Rivera* and the children! Kill every last one!"

His cry was answered by a dozen gunshots. The mounted Roadrunner horses surged forward. Mundo's chestnut crushed against the rest. When another horse tripped and fell against his mare, he lost his balance. His musket sling slipped over his head and the gun fell off.

It took a minute to regain control of the chestnut. In a blur Mundo could see distant guns and gray-uniformed men rushing through the dusk, firing at cowboys he'd known since he was a baby.

An instant later, the Roadrunner foreman tumbled off his horse.

A terrible roar came out of *Papá*'s mouth. He spurred his gelding directly toward the Texans. A gray-clad trooper dropped to one knee and took direct aim.

"Papá!" Mundo yelled, not sure if it was a warning or a plea.

Then the shots began to shriek through the trees, one after another and some at the same time. Mundo screamed for his father again and again, but *Papá* had disappeared in the smoke and falling darkness. *Don* Victor galloped after him. Mundo could hear men shouting and shooting and swearing as they disappeared. But the foreman did not move. He lay in a shattered lump.

Without thinking, Mundo jumped off his horse and knelt beside the loyal old man. He pressed his fingers to the side of the sunleathered neck, but he felt no pulse. He laid his head on the foreman's heart, but he heard nothing.

There was no hint of life at all.

Mundo's mind went numb. His stomach heaved. And then he started shaking.

Another shot shattered the low branch of a piñon pine, terrifying his mare. The chestnut reared and ripped its lead from Mundo's hand. Blindly he stared at the beast, then at the dead foreman, acutely aware that his father had abandoned him.

Mundo had left the Roadrunner determined to prove himself as a soldier defending his beloved land, but suddenly he knew he was a only a boy, dismounted, unarmed, and alone in what had become the enemy's country.

To his shame, he ran.

He ran from the ringing bullets and the shouting men. He ran through sumac and scraggly junipers. He ran until the galloping of his heart began to crush his airless lungs.

He could not breathe. He could not stop. He could not go on.

But still he ran. He ran and leaped and fell and rolled and crawled to his feet and ran again. He ran until he could no longer hear the brutal gasps of men or the terrifying screams of dying horses. He ran until he knew, until he was certain, that he would never have to face an enemy soldier again.

Finally he darted behind a huge chunk of granite that was framed by a pair of massive firs. It was not a real cave, but he pretended it was. It was the closest thing to shelter Mundo could find.

Struggling for air, he clung to one tall trunk. He took a dozen desperate gulps, still terrified but feeling almost sane. Maybe he'd survived the battle. Maybe he'd escaped. Maybe his *Papá* had—

And then he heard a moan. Mundo's head snapped around so fast that a pain ripped through his lock-tight neck. Again his heart began to pound.

He was facing a blue-eyed, shaggy-haired boy in his late teens, half-bent over and close to collapse. Despite the cold, his torn military-issue jacket hung open against his scrawny frame, revealing smoke-smeared, red-stained long johns and the unmistakable striped gray pants of an enemy soldier.

His carbine, scuffed and scarred, was pointed at Mundo's face.

Chapter Five

"Don't you dare move. Don't you even breathe," Private Riley ordered the terrified Hispanic boy.

The kid stood as still as a nest-sitting mother bird, his eyes huge and shocked. Riley realized that, even if he'd wanted to, the boy couldn't budge.

Riley was relieved. In the first place, he'd seen more bloody, mangled bodies in the past few days than he'd ever imagined he would see in his lifetime, and he didn't want to shoot somebody else tonight. In the second place, his side hurt so much that it took all his might to aim and steady the heavy carbine. He wasn't sure he could find the strength to fire it as well.

He rocked slightly on his feet. Minutes ago he'd caught an enemy bullet from a passing cowboy and crawled off behind the rocks to see where he was hit. Mercifully, the minié ball had not shattered his ribs. Still, he was bleeding heavily and getting woozier by the second. It was only a matter of time before Riley's prisoner realized he was too weak to hold his carbine.

"You speak English?" he asked.

The boy did not answer.

Wearily Riley switched into Spanish. He was not fluent in the way of the silver-tongued merchants of San Antonio, but he'd grown up in South Texas and could speak border Spanish as well as most Gulf Coast fishermen.

"How big is your unit?" he asked in what he assumed was the boy's native tongue. "How far away is your base camp?"

The boy looked startled, but still he did not speak. Riley was getting angry. He wanted to resolve this—to do *something* with his captive—before he fell right at the boy's feet. Or the boy lunged at him and took the gun.

"Why aren't you armed?" he asked belatedly.

Now the boy looked down, no longer frightened, but ashamed. It occurred to Riley that maybe the boy wasn't a soldier after all. He had no weapon, and he reeked of fear. Of course, Riley had found himself in the same situation more than once since he'd left Texas, and he knew that most of the New Mexicans had not been issued arms or uniforms.

"You gonna answer me?" he asked, trying to threaten the boy with his carbine. It was a lost cause. The tiny effort of lifting the barrel half an inch coincided with another wave of nausea. Riley's knees crumpled and he fell.

In an instant, the boy was on him. His clenched fist came down on Riley's jaw almost before he dropped the gun. Riley tried to block the blow, but his hands were shaky and his judgment impaired. He reached for the boy's throat, but the boy slugged him again, in the stomach this time. Instinctively Riley shielded his bleeding side as the boy hit him again and again.

Now, at last, the boy was talking. No—he was shouting, in Spanish, shouting things that made no sense.

"You killed *Mamá!* You killed my brothers! My father will die because of you! You will never reach my sister! Never! Julio will not have to shoot you down! *I will kill you first! I will kill you all!*"

He kept on hollering as he slammed his fists into Riley. Riley curled up in pain, his wound freshly bloodied by the blows. He felt faint. He could not think. He could barely lift his arms to protect himself.

"The Roadrunner Ranch is Rivera land! *My* land! No Texan will ever set foot upon it again! Never, do you hear me?"

Riley had grown up having to defend himself with his fists, and in some other place and time, this fight would not have fazed him. But he was terribly wounded, and he was at war. He knew that if he didn't manage to fight back, and soon, the boy would beat him senseless and grab his gun.

That's when he realized that the carbine lay beside the two of them. The other boy was far too close for Riley to draw on, but he'd been taught to use a weapon in more ways than one.

When Mundo came to it was dark, black-as-death dark, and he could not remember where he was or why there was a hideous pounding inside his head.

He did not move. He was not sure that he could. He felt shaken, deep-down shaken, in a way that seemed to him greater than the way he'd felt the time he'd been trampled by a bull. Something seemed to be broken. Not in his body, but in his heart.

"I got my eye on you, Yankee, so don't even twitch."

The voice came out of the darkness. At first, Mundo didn't think the Texan—the speaker could be from nowhere but Texas with that drawl—was talking to him. After all, Mundo was *not* a Yankee. But as the memory of the terrible battle swept back over him, he realized that he could take no chances.

He straightened slightly, unable to stop the throbbing in his head. Abruptly he remembered the last thing that had happened before he'd found himself wrapped in blackness. Someone—this fellow?—had slammed a gun butt against his skull.

"Hard luck, Yankee. We both passed out. But I came to first. And I've still got the gun."

When Mundo didn't answer, the Texan said, "I forgot. You don't speak English." He switched to Mundo's native tongue. "You do understand I'm holding a fully loaded repeater to your head? Ain't much chance I could miss with all those bullets waitin'."

Mundo understood, in English and in Spanish. Like every Hispanic boy of the highest class, he'd been tutored in literature and arithmetic since his tender years. He wanted to brag to this soldier boy, to point out his superior breeding and education, but some cautious part of him held back. The boy spoke Spanish poorly, but he could be understood. Maybe Mundo could learn something if he at least kept his knowledge of the Texan's language to himself.

"I understand," Mundo answered in Spanish. His head still ached unbearably. "But I do not understand why you keep calling me a Yankee. I am Rai*mundo* Carlos Esteban Rivera y Gonzales—" the ghost of five generations of Roadrunner wealth and reputation echoed in his squeaky voice, "and my family has lived in this country since the time it was first claimed by Spain."

The Texan laughed. "Well, *la-ti-da!*" he ridiculed Mundo. His drawl seemed exaggerated, slow and sleepy, before he switched back to Spanish. "No wonder you fellows can't win a war. You don't even know which side you're on. Now me—" country pride swelled his low tone, "I'm fightin' for Texas. And Texas is fightin' for the Confederacy. *You're* fightin' *me.* That makes *you* a Yankee, 'cause Yankees is who started this whole dang thing."

Mundo's stomach tightened. "We fought the Yankees when they stole our land from Mexico," he protested. "But that's all over. They run things now. We don't like them much, but we don't hate them anywhere close to the way we hate Texans."

This time the silence was grim, and he wondered if he'd gone too far. He was angry, angry at everyone and everything, but he was also scared. In hindsight he realized that he should be the one holding the carbine. If he'd been thinking like a soldier instead of a schoolboy bent on revenge . . .

"You can hate us all you want, but one Texan can whup a dozen Yankees, so y'all don't got no chance." The Texan's voice sounded very shaky for somebody doing so much bragging. "We're gonna show them Yankees that they can't take over Texas. We're—"

"I don't see anybody taking over Texas," Mundo countered sharply. "All I see is a bunch of filthy Texans trying to run over *us*."

In the darkness, he heard the carbine's hammer cock. He thought of his father, who had ridden blindly into battle. He thought of his mother, whom he had never really known. He thought of Chayito, waiting at the ranch, and knew that Julio would bravely defend his sister and the wedding guests. But the Roadrunner no longer had enough men to protect its people. When the Texans had shot them down . . .

Chayito's face filled his mind, and he could not finish the thought.

"I was gonna turn you over to my sergeant," the Texan threatened in a strangled gasp, "but if I gotta put up with your mouth I don't think it's worth the trouble. You got any reason why I shouldn't just blast you away?"

Half of Mundo wanted to tell him he didn't care, to go ahead and shoot: he would be proud to die for his country. But the other half of him was begging, *Don't shoot me. I don't want to die.*

"Yes, I have a reason," he blurted suddenly. "A very good reason you should keep me alive."

~~~

As the fire dwindled down inside the circle of rocks, Tenchi considered her best chance of escape. It was, she knew, a miracle that she had convinced the Texan outlaw—she'd learned his name was Toland—not to kill her. But it was more important that he, in turn, had convinced his partner—or was Kurtzer his boss?—that taking her along was worth the great profit Tenchi promised.

She *was* worth a lot of money. That much was true. But only major trade merchants or wealthy ranchers like *El Patrón* generally purchased weavers in New Mexico. Nobody else could afford them. And it was rare that rustlers—what other name was there for these men?— were on good terms with such people.

Of course, there was a lot she did not yet know about this gang of outlaws, though since last night she had learned all she could. Because she was a girl, they had assumed that she was a good cook. She had not told them otherwise, because cooking gave her a reason to move around freely, to eavesdrop on their conversation as they settled down around the fire. And they seemed satisfied with what she'd fed them, which meant they had survived on pitiful rations for far too long.

Tenchi had never learned how to cook well because she had rarely been allowed in an owner's kitchen. She had been forbidden to go to lots of places. One of her owners had refused to let her near his gun racks, or his barn.

He needn't have worried. Since the night of her capture, Tenchi had never held a firearm and only twice had she mounted a horse. The last thing she intended to do was try to steal one.

The outlaws, however, seemed intent on seizing every horse in New Mexico. Tenchi had learned where they'd come from and what they planned to do. She had also discovered that every day they split into small groups to cover more territory. Each night they brought back whatever they'd stolen and hid the animals in this narrow, limestone canyon.

The animals drank from a half-hidden spring. Nobody, just riding by, would ever guess how much room there was in the back of the canyon, or how much water.

The outlaws were nearly done with this part of New Mexico. Tonight they were waiting for Kurtzer and Toland, who'd gone off to raid Albuquerque. Tomorrow they planned to head due east, away from the fighting, toward the bone-dry Staked Plains. Tenchi did not know what they would do about water when they left this canyon, or what she would do about it herself. She had only a few hours left to solve the problem, however, because she planned to vanish the moment Kurtzer and Toland showed up, covering her escape with the arrival of a noisy herd of horses.

Chapter Six

If he hadn't been so weak, Riley would have laughed out loud when the Hispanic boy told his silly story about belonging to one of New Mexico's finest families. He said he was worth a king's ransom to his father, or his big brother, or whoever it was running things back at the ranch. Roadrunner, he called it. Bar Double R. Since there were more roadrunners in New Mexico than cattle, it wouldn't be hard for a local to make that up.

The kid was all together too—well, fancy—for Riley's taste. He'd shown up for a battle dressed sweet and sharp, as though he were on his way to church. His eyes were dark and his clear skin had a healthy glow. And he spoke such prissy Spanish! Claimed to have been tutored by some famous guy from Spain. Riley didn't know too many people who'd gone to school at all, let alone got their learning from somebody special. If their ma or pa knew some arithmetic and how to read the

Bible, they were doing all right. Riley didn't know how to do either one.

Then again, he didn't know who his ma or pa were, not for sure. And what he guessed didn't set too well with him.

As night settled in for good, Riley began to wish he'd just shot the kid when he'd first seen him. The fist fight had set his wound to bleeding even more fiercely. By now Riley was far too woozy to cope with anybody, friend or foe. He wanted nothing more than to lie down somewhere and let night fill him with peace and the fragile hope that maybe, somehow, he'd be better by morning. He pushed away the soldier's truth—that he'd probably be dead by then.

When a nighthawk trilled from beneath a nearby cholla, Riley abruptly became aware that he was drifting, that the boy was probably waiting for him to fade off so he could run. Half of Riley didn't care. An enemy soldier had to be stopped, killed, or captured, but he wasn't even sure this boy was a soldier, and as long as Riley held the gun, the boy couldn't hurt him.

He was nodding off again when he heard the Hispanic kid's furtive footsteps. Somehow Riley roused himself.

"Stop! Not another step!"

There was a painful silence. Then the boy said in Spanish, "I'm not moving."

The moon had come up since Riley had dozed off and he could see that his captive had already gone twenty yards. "Back this way, slow and steady, arms raised."

"You know I'm not armed," the boy countered.

"Do it anyway."

A moment later he heard an odd thump. "It's a *body*," the Rivera boy announced in an eerie voice. "I tripped over a body!"

Riley didn't answer. He was certain now that this boy had not been to war long, or at all, if he was still counting bodies in the dark. Riley had long since ceased to notice them.

Suddenly the Hispanic boy squeaked, "It's moving!"

"Of course I'm moving," growled a man's voice. "I was just standin' here and you tripped over me, you fool."

It was the voice of a Texan who sounded old enough—and arrogant enough—to be a Confederate officer.

Riley straightened. He would have saluted but he couldn't do it and still aim his gun.

"I'm sorry, sir. Private Riley, sir, First Regiment. He's my prisoner. I was waiting for someone to come for him."

There was a strange silence. Riley tried to get a good look at the fellow in the moonlight. He was young for an officer. He had a small mouth and seemed to be missing a tooth. He bore no insignia and his uniform was as ragged as Riley's.

"Uh, why didn't you just take him back to, uh, camp, soldier?"

It was a good question, the one Riley had hoped to avoid. "I've been shot, sir. I don't think I can walk very far. I don't know how much longer I can hold a gun on him."

"Well, he's your prisoner. Find a way to deal with him. I got other things to do."

"But, sir," Riley protested, a bit mystified by the soldier's attitude, "I might . . . I might lose him any time. I've lost a lot of blood—"

"Then shoot him. He's the enemy."

Riley heard the Hispanic boy gasp. For all his bravado, he *was* afraid. Riley couldn't blame him. He'd seen Texan troops gun down enemy soldiers—and Texan deserters—without a moment's grace.

"Uh . . . that may not be the best idea, sir," Riley said hesitantly. "He may be worth a lot of money to us."

"Us?" the voice rasped sharply.

"The Confederacy, sir." Riley was feeling uneasy. It was hard to say how men might act after a hard skirmish. This one might be injured, or shell-shocked, or exhausted, or hiding grief. But he wasn't acting like an officer, at least not any of the ones Riley had known. Wanting to kill an enemy was one thing, especially in battle. But this man had not suggested shooting the Hispanic kid with any heat. He just wanted the whole problem out of the way. And what Texan soldier asked what another one meant by "us?" "Us" and "them" was what made a war a war. Riley—and the other soldier—were on the side of Texas, the Rebel South, the Confederacy. The enemy was any abolitionist, any Yankee, anybody who supported gorilla-faced Lincoln's Union.

"He's rich," Riley offered, not sure why it mattered to him. He owed nothing to the Hispanic braggart. But right was right and wrong was wrong. Killing the boy in battle would have been right. But it didn't make sense to shoot him now, when he offered no resistance and was merely in the way.

"How can he be rich? He's just a kid."

"He's the son of the wealthiest man in New Mexico," Riley answered, exaggerating the Rivera kid's story just a bit. "I bet the Yankees would trade a hundred of our men in exchange for this one prisoner."

Again the odd silence. "Or they'd pay for him? Or his rich daddy would?"

"Yes, sir," Riley answered. "He gave me to believe that his pa would pay any price for his safe return." That much was certainly true. Riley hadn't swallowed whole the boy's strutting, that's for sure. But the kid had made the claim. And if somebody gave him the chance, Riley was sure he'd make it again.

"Is that true, boy?" the man barked in the direction of Riley's captive. "You worth a mint?"

"He don't speak no English," Riley explained. "Speaks fancy-pants Spanish, but—"

"If he don't speak English, how do you know all this? You playin' with me, boy?"

"No, sir!" Riley insisted. "I grew up with Mexican fishermen. I learned Spanish from—"

"Never mind. You sure he's who he says he is?"

Now it was Riley's turn to be silent. He'd started down this trail to get rid of his troublesome prisoner, then to keep him alive. Now he realized that he was vouching for a stranger who'd beaten him up.

He was too woozy to think, or even stand up much longer. The pain was growing unbearable.

In Spanish, he said to the boy, "Did you tell me the truth? As God is your witness, is your father that rich?"

With less fear than haughtiness, the boy replied,

"You are not fit to wipe his cowbarn boots."

That confirmed it for Riley. "See what I mean, sir? I done lived with Mexicans all my life. They don't talk all uppity like that. This one comes from people who drip with money. You can tell it from his voice."

"Yeah, I reckon you can," the other man said slowly. "Where's he say his daddy lives? Somewhere close by?"

"He called his land Roadrunner Ranch, sir."

The small-mouthed man grinned. "Heir to the Roadrunner fortune, eh? We'll give it a shot, run it by the boss."

Riley assumed he meant his commanding officer, although the men more often called him "the old man" than "the boss."

"Thank you, sir. And I'd be grateful if you'd send a medic back for me when you have the time." Riley was ready to pass out. "Unless it would be best for me to fall in with your unit. I don't—"

"Toland, what's takin' so long?" boomed out a new voice from the direction of the battlefield.

Riley turned to gaze at the second man. The moon shone on his dirty face. He had a long, jagged scar on one cheek. He looked maybe twenty years older than Toland.

"Got us a hostage, Kurtzer," said the first man. "Rich boy worth—"

"Not another kid! Toland, we got to ride, ride hard. We can't be towing along these natives you think we can sell." The second man's voice was ugly and harsh. "Let's just stick to horses."

"Come on, Kurtzer. The boy says he's from the

Roadrunner. It's only fair that we get some more profit from that ranch," he wheedled. "Besides, this is such easy money."

Riley was certain now that he couldn't be an officer. No Texas officer *ever* begged.

"You said that about the Navajo girl."

"Well, she ain't been no trouble. At least we got us some decent grub."

"We don't know if we can sell her, either," the man named Kurtzer grumbled back. "I ain't never tried blackmail or kidnapping. They only taught us how to shoot and 'forage' in the army."

By now Riley was confused. The two were up to something, something wrong, but they sounded like Texan soldiers, too. By his way of thinking, how could a man be fighting for the Confederacy and not be right and moral?

A second question plagued him too. If they couldn't get ransom for the Rivera boy, what would they do with him?

"The Texan boy wants to ride with us," said Toland. "We could use another gun."

"Now that's a great idea," said Kurtzer sarcastically. "All we need is *three* kids instead of—"

"Well, it's not such a bad idea," countered Toland. "What else are we gonna do with him? He's seen us both—"

"Then get rid of him. We got horses to collect. Them that didn't get shot on the battlefield."

Riley didn't know what to do. These men didn't

belong to a real Texas unit! They were scavengers. They spoke of killing humans as though they were mule deer. It wasn't right to turn a prisoner over to them. They were sure to kill the rich kid! They were even threatening to kill Riley.

Riley couldn't help looking at the Hispanic boy. The boy's chin was proud, a touch too high, but his black eyes were wide and almost misty.

Riley wasn't surprised the boy was scared. But he *was* surprised that he was looking back at him like that—Riley still held a gun on him—as though he were asking for help.

Begging, more like it.

He knows as well as I do that these two would just as soon see him dead, Riley realized. He tried to think of the other boy as an enemy soldier, but he couldn't get past the sense that he was a boy, just another boy, a boy just like himself.

They were both in terrible trouble. Only Riley could get them out.

"Well, what do you say?" he asked the outlaws as cheerfully as he could manage. "Could I ride along with you?" He tried to look eager and naive.

Kurtzer muttered something under his breath.

"Don't seem right to shoot no Texas boy," commented Toland. "Besides, we're short-handed. And I still think the easy way to money is—"

"I'm tired of listening to what you think, Toland. I want to get on with business and get back to Texas."

"So do I, but that don't mean we oughtta shoot

every kid we see! The ones I scored is worth a lot more alive to us than dead. You know, like beef on the hoof."

"Oh, all right," Kurtzer snapped. "Let the Rebel boy come along. But if he doesn't measure up or gets outta line, Toland, it's on your head." He turned to Riley. "You're in charge of the prisoner till we get where we're going tonight. Don't cross me. *Not ever.* If you know how to follow orders, we might let you join us."

Stiffly, Riley nodded. He was close to fainting, and his jacket was soaked with blood.

Chapter Seven

Mundo was scared, deep-down-in-the-pit-of-his-stomach scared, in a way he had never been before. His heart was throbbing as well as his head.

He didn't see any chance of escape, but he did what he could to help himself. He took note of the position of the moon as they headed east, and he mentally made note of his mount's brand—the Roadrunner's Bar Double R!—and the number of horses. Probably a dozen. Most of them looked too sleek and fat to have spent much time with the army.

To his right rode the Texan boy who was responsible for all of this, slouching on his own buckskin gelding and carrying his own carbine. Mundo wasn't sure whether to be mad at him or grateful. He also wasn't sure why the outlaw named Kurtzer had given in to the one named Toland. Toland didn't seem to have any muscle, any strength. He'd just whined a bit. It was confusing.

Private Riley's behavior had been confusing, too. The other men were obviously outlaws of some kind, which in Mundo's mind was pretty much the basic description of Texas soldiers. But Riley had stopped them from killing him.

And that wasn't all. Riley was wounded, so weak and wobbly that Mundo had nearly escaped from him. He'd admitted as much to the outlaws, but they had ignored his problems. Once he'd realized they weren't part of the Texas army, Riley had never mentioned his gunshot wound again.

Yet Mundo could see fresh dark liquid heavily staining his Confederate jacket. Riley weaved and bobbled on his horse, and it wasn't because of the rocky ground or rising wind. Finally he pulled off his carbine—the sling was rubbing against his blood-soaked chest—and looped the strap tightly around his saddle horn. Mundo had never seen a soldier do such a thing. The Texas boy must be feeling even worse than he looked.

Riley slumped in the saddle for a good three hours, but he managed to stay on the buckskin. At last they rode up a steep bluff into a narrow, piñon-studded canyon and stopped. Toland was at the front of the group, but it was Kurtzer who let out a low whistle. As Mundo heard an answer, he spotted a campfire hidden behind some rocks and scrubby trees. Nearby he could hear the restless sounds of dozens—maybe hundreds—of horses.

A whistle came back to them. In a moment, two men appeared on foot.

"It's about time! We thought we'd lost you fellows."

With no expression, Toland said, "Three of our men got killed this morning, down in Albuquerque."

He mentioned their names, which meant nothing to Mundo. Apparently they didn't mean much to the other men, either, because none of them commented on the group's loss.

"Locals didn't want to share," Kurtzer explained. "Fortunately, the soldiers was more accomodatin'."

"You stole army horses? Are you nuts?" one of the bandits asked.

"No, we stumbled into a skirmish and found fat stock running loose. Fresh from local ranchers. Just luck."

Mundo seethed. *Papá* had disappeared in that battle! The Roadrunner had lost many good men. This stolen herd included Roadrunner stock. Kurtzer spoke of the deadly skirmish as though it were a game!

"Lots of New Mexican cowboys. Texan troops got most of them, and when they were done, we just sauntered in and rounded up the horses."

Mundo's fists tightened, but somehow he stayed still while all the men laughed.

"That don't explain where you picked up these young pups."

"It was Toland's idea," Kurtzer muttered. "Says we can hold one for ransom and let the other ride with us."

By now Mundo was barely listening. He'd spotted something odd—a furtive movement near the campfire. Hope pounded in his chest. It might be somebody from the Roadrunner! Surely his family would send someone to rescue him . . . once they figured out where he was.

But how would they know unless his kidnappers

contacted them with a demand? He shuddered at the thought of these bandits riding anywhere near his home.

The wind was growing more brisk. One man stepped forward, his face stern in the fuzzy moonlight.

"Kurtzer, how many times can you pay him back for savin' your life?"

It was a girl. It had to be a girl because Mundo could see the graceful sway of a long yellow skirt. She was dressed like a poor Hispanic . . . or a rich one's servant. Either way, he could not imagine what a girl was doing with a rough bunch like this unless she was, well, not very nice.

Or unless she had no choice.

She was wearing a blue-and-red blanket with a slit down the middle for her head. A black *rebozo* hid most of her hair. But as she turned toward the outlaws for just a moment, Mundo caught a glimpse of her round, coppery face.

She was a Navajo.

Without warning, she began to run. Silently she bolted away from the gathered men, her moccasined feet all but flying over the rocks and underbrush as she raced toward the narrow mouth of the canyon.

The rustlers who stood with their backs to her did not notice, but as Kurtzer reached for his canteen, he briefly faced in her direction. "Hey!" he shouted. "What's that?"

"The girl!" Toland answered. "The Indian!"

"Stop her!" yelled another one of the outlaws. "She's worth a lot!"

"And she knows too much!"

At once Toland pulled out his revolver. Before he could fire, Riley spurred the buckskin in Toland's direction and kneed his horse into Toland's as he reached out to knock Toland's gun from his hand. He was too weak to loosen Toland's grasp, but he did manage to make the shot go wild.

"You got no call to kill no innocent girl!" Riley hollered.

Mundo was shocked. He hadn't even been sure Riley was still conscious. Why would he risk any more trouble with this bunch for a Navajo?

Maybe he doesn't know any better, Mundo thought. *Poor fool Texan probably doesn't even know the difference between the friendly Pueblo Indians and the deadly Navajos.* Every New Mexican did. Mundo had been taught from the cradle that Navajos could never be trusted.

It took Toland only a second to knock Riley out with the butt of his revolver, another second for Riley to crumple like half-burned kindling and roll slowly out of his saddle. In the meantime, Kurtzer broke his mount past the group, shook out his lariat, and lassoed the Navajo girl like a wet-nosed spring calf. He half-led, half-dragged her back to the group of outlaws. Wildly thrashing against the rope, she crashed heavily into one, then another, before Kurtzer jerked the rope so hard she fell to the ground.

Chapter Eight

Hours later, Tenchi watched as the Texan boy lay half-conscious in the dirt where he had fallen, sweating profusely and shivering at the same time. She was not sure what he had done to upset the outlaws. She'd heard a commotion as she tried to escape and, after she was roped, she'd seen him lying on the ground.

He had obviously lost a great deal of blood—she could see that he was still bleeding—and even if the outlaws left him alive when they pulled out in the morning, he was too weak to gather food. He was surely too shaky to crawl down to the muddy spring where the horses drank and bathed.

The Texan's buckskin gelding had wandered off in that direction shortly after Tenchi had feigned her slip and "crashed" into a rustler with a knife poking out of its sheath. With all her deliberate writhing, no one had noticed that she'd grabbed it and tucked it into her knee-high moccasin just moments before she'd been slammed to the ground.

It had been years since she'd been treated so badly by her captors, and Tenchi's indignity flared along with her fear. There had been a time—more than one time—when she'd found a measure of peace with her weaving after being purchased by a decent family. Mrs. Sampson, her third owner's wife, had been the wife of a Yankee officer who was often away from the fort. She had been good to Tenchi, making sure she had fresh straw in her pallet, nursing her when she was ill, and secretly leaving sweet treats where Tenchi could find them. At that time Tenchi had been too young to know the difference between the way a white person treats a child and the way she treats a favorite slave. Homesick and frightened, she was simply grateful for Mrs. Sampson's warmth.

But Mrs. Sampson had died after a year in New Mexico, and her husband had sold Tenchi as soon as he'd been assigned to another post. Years had passed before Tenchi had been purchased by another kindly soul.

Pushing the memories from her mind, Tenchi wondered if anybody had gone to collect the Texan boy's buckskin. She might be able to get away on a saddled horse! Since she no longer had surprise in her favor, she would need great speed to escape.

It was so windy in the canyon that she knew the land below would be swirling with dust devils tonight. She needed to head toward the one place the outlaws wouldn't want to go. What Texas horsethief would brave a genuine New Mexican dust storm to chase a Navajo

girl who might be worth a little extra spending money?
The bandits had collected lots of superb, well-fed horses.
They had the rich boy. They didn't need her.

Yes, that plan might work. She would have to cut
loose her wrists and ankles without anybody seeing her.
That would be hard. But nobody knew she had the
knife. And she only had to worry about the rustlers.
After all, the Hispanic boy, tied to a neighboring cypress,
had problems of his own, and the Texan was as good as
dead right now.

Riley thought he fell asleep for awhile. He was too
groggy to care. As he came to, he realized he was lying
near the Navajo girl, whose ankles were tied together
with a long rope that wound around the trunk of a
nearby tree. Her hands were tied behind her. The Hispanic kid, similarly bound, was sitting up, face expres-
sionless, refusing to look at anyone.

Vaguely Riley became aware of the pain in his side,
the dizziness in his head, and weakness of his entire
body. The outlaws had not bothered to tie him up. That
was good news, but it also meant they thought he was
too weak to pose any threat to them. Riley knew they
were right.

The wind battered his face with tiny leaves and sand.
It also carried the outlaws' voices toward Riley. They were
speaking English, so he had no trouble understanding

them. He knew that the Spanish-speaking boy couldn't follow the words, but he wasn't sure about the girl.

"Dang fool pup! Thought *I* was an officer!" howled Toland. "I told him to just shoot the prisoner."

Kurtzer, the one who seemed to be in charge, added, "The Texas boy convinced Toland the Hispanic kid was worth a mint. He talked us into letting him ride with us, too."

"Yeah, Kurtzer, and you do whatever Toland wants," teased another man.

Kurtzer's voice grew hard. "I do whatever *I* want. And I like the easy road to all that cash."

A few of the outlaws chuckled uncertainly. To Riley, it was a chilling sound.

Then one of them said darkly, "I still say we should just get rid of 'em."

After a cold silence, another man grunted. "I agree. When you said to pick the territory clean, Kurtzer, you weren't talkin' about Navajo slaves and ransomed children. And that Texan kid don't even know what side he's on. We got enough to worry about. We don't need that rich boy's daddy riding after us."

A third man nodded. "It's just not worth the trouble."

After that, nobody spoke for a while. Riley secretly watched the bandits, hoping he might pick up some clue to help himself out of this predicament. One of them roughly threw a log on the fire, causing a spray of sparks. Another walked toward the herd to stand guard.

Finally the one called Kurtzer spoke. "I think we've got to go with the boys on this one, Toland. When I agreed to bring along the girl, I didn't think she'd run. And I sure didn't think that Texas boy would try to jump us."

"Yeah, neither did I," agreed Toland. "Ungrateful little whelp."

Again they laughed awkwardly together. Riley shivered at the sound.

Then Kurtzer ordered, "This whole mess is your fault, Toland. Shoot 'em before we pull out in the morning."

Mundo watched, and listened, and watched some more. As the wind picked up above the canyon and the temperature dropped inside it, he grew almost stiff with the cold. He had no shelter, and no way to get some. He had no ally and no weapon.

He had no plan.

The men were rolling out bedrolls, propping up their saddles like oversized pillows. None of them had paid much attention to the three kids in a while. Private Riley lay where he'd fallen, asleep or unconscious since he'd been knocked flat by Toland. But the girl ... the girl was as alert as a hunted doe.

She had a knife. Mundo had seen her slip it into her moccasin. It was the only weapon he could possibly get his hands on.

He looked at the Navajo, really looked at her. *She* was

watching, waiting, just as he was. To the men at the fire, her body looked perfectly still beneath the blue-and-red blanket. But from Mundo's angle, it was obvious that her hands, tied behind her back, were edging toward her knee.

She was going for the knife.

"I can get it," he whispered in Spanish.

She jerked, eyes wide open, and stared at his face.

"I can reach the knife. Just slide your legs over here. Slowly." He would never have thought of touching her moccasin, let alone her knee, if the girl had been of his own social class. But she was, after all, an Indian.

Nervously, the Navajo glanced at Private Riley, who did not move, then back toward the men by the fire.

"I saw you steal it. I know what you're doing," Mundo threatened. "If you want to get out of here, you'll give me that knife."

"So you can escape and leave me here?"

"So I can escape and give the knife back to you. Otherwise I'll tell the outlaws you've got a weapon hidden."

"You won't give the knife back! You'll take it with you."

Mundo had not really thought of what he'd do with the weapon once he escaped. The girl was a Navajo, not a person. The honor of a Rivera's word did not apply to Indians.

"I will not live any longer as a slave!" Fury lashed her voice. "I *will* find a way to escape. You will not stop me."

"I'm not trying to stop you!" he barked. "I don't care what you do after I'm free. I just want to get out of here alive."

She did not answer, but neither did she move.

"I help you cut your ropes. You help me cut mine. We go in silence. We go our own ways."

Mundo could see anger flood her face. "You will slow me down! You will give me away!"

This time it was Mundo who reddened. "I am a sixth-generation Rivera!" he snapped. "I have lived here all my life. I could ride before I could walk. These Texan fools may cower in a true New Mexico dust storm, but *I* will survive."

They stared at each other, both tied, both determined, as each judged the price of collaboration ... and freedom. Neither would look away.

They both jerked abruptly when a shaky voice came from the ground nearby.

"Get on with it. Both of you. Don't you dare waste time fightin' with each other." It was Riley. Not dead, not sleeping, but tenaciously awake. He coughed with the effort of speaking. "I'm goin' with you. I swear by all that's holy, I'll holler if you try to leave without me. I ain't got nothin' to lose."

Chapter Nine

In the dark, Riley could see nothing, but he could hear tiny sawing sounds. The Rivera boy had gotten hold of the knife first, and spent an endless amount of time working on his ankles. Once he was free, he crawled ever so silently over to the girl.

He was giving her the knife when Riley dozed off. When he woke up an hour later, both of them had freed their wrists, the girl's feet were still bound, and they were arguing again. It was hard for Riley to make out their fast, whispered Spanish.

"If I get the horses now, you'll be done by the time I get back!" the boy said.

"If you get the horses now, you'll just take off and leave me here. They'll hear you. By the time I'm done cutting my ropes, I won't have a chance!"

Neither one of them, Riley noticed, appeared to be concerned about him.

"You're saying I should just sit here while you cut yourself free? Do nothing? Then we both go to the herd and—"

"No," the girl insisted. "I'm getting that Texas boy's horse. It's still down by the spring. It's got a saddle on it. And a gun."

"Take whatever horse you want. But I'm going to cut one out now. It takes a while when you're on foot and have no halter, especially when it's dark and you have to make no sound. If I—"

At last Riley roused himself to speak. "Ain't you two forgettin' something? I ain't dead yet."

Awkward silence filled the space between them.

"There's nothing I can do for you right now," the girl defended herself in English. "Until I get the buckskin—"

"I could get it sooner," the Hispanic boy cut her off. "I could catch your horse, Texan, and have it ready before she's even done with her ropes. But she—"

"Go get my horse, Rich Boy," Riley ordered. He had no reason to take the other boy's side, but the Rivera kid's hands and feet were already untied. The sooner he caught Riley's buckskin, the sooner Riley would be free. He might yet make it out of this canyon.

To the girl he said, "When your feet are loose, you go catch one from the herd."

The Rivera boy stood up, very slowly, as though to ease the cramps of long-still legs.

Before he could take a step, the girl begged Riley, "I have to have your horse. The one by the spring."

His temper rose. "We're trying to save our lives! This is no time to argue about horses!"

"You don't understand," she pleaded. "I can't catch an unsaddled horse. I can't even ride one!"

"She's lying," the Hispanic boy cut in. "Navajos are born stealing horses."

"I haven't lived with my people since I was eight!" she confessed, her voice hoarse and almost tearful. "I remember some things, but not others. I can ride when I have to, but . . . it's been a very long time since I went out on my own and caught an untethered horse."

Riley believed her. He didn't know why. He had no reason to trust the Indian. It was stupid to give in to her.

Stupider yet to miss a chance to escape by fighting over details.

"You go to the herd and cut out a horse for yourself," he said to Rivera. "When she's done she can go fetch mine. I'll probably need somebody to keep me from falling off anyway." He turned to the girl. "I'm too weak to walk, so I'll be takin' the buckskin—and my carbine—once we're safely out of here. That's the deal."

"Of course." Her voice was half-mad, half-grateful. He wasn't used to the Navajo accent, so it was hard to tell.

"I'll make my way to the mouth of the canyon and wait for you there. If either one of you tries to leave this place before I'm safely mounted, you'll never make it down that bluff before I tip off the bandits. Do you understand?"

The girl said irritably, "I understand."

The boy said nothing before he melted off.

After that, Riley waited. He listened to the girl cut at her ropes, and he waited. He strained to listen to the horses, to any sound that might alert the rustlers standing guard. He could hear nothing that hinted that the rich boy had reached the herd.

At last, he heard the girl give a tiny gasp of triumph. Quickly, gracefully, she stood up.

"Don't try to leave without me," Riley warned before she slipped away.

It didn't take Mundo long to reach the horses. It bothered him that he, the son of the richest man in his valley, was actually being forced to steal livestock! Then he remembered that some of these horses were Roadrunner stock, so he wouldn't really be stealing. Any horse with a Roadrunner brand belonged to him. And any horse with *El Patrón*'s brand . . . well, he hoped he wouldn't find one.

Swiftly, silently, he crept toward the herd, hand outstretched as though he had sugar or an apple. The first horse shied sideways. The second one trotted away from him. Three more ducked when they spotted Mundo. Finally, in exasperation, he lunged at one.

He caught only the tips of the long mane, but it was enough. The sorrel didn't like having its hair pulled any more than Mundo did. It stopped just long enough for him to step closer, get a good handful of mane, and then, as Julio had taught him years ago, to leap up on the horse.

Without a sound he nudged the sorrel to the far side of the canyon, putting as much distance as possible between himself and the sleeping men. He couldn't see any outlaws guarding the herd, and that troubled him.

Men had to be posted somewhere. Mundo didn't want to accidentally trip over them.

Still, he had to go. He didn't know if Riley had made it to the mouth of the canyon yet, and he couldn't afford to care. His life—his family's life—was at stake. He could take no more chances.

Silently he pressed the sorrel along the north canyon wall, past the juneberry and skunkbrush where it was unlikely any bandit would be waiting. The night was perfectly quiet. If his luck held until he reached the mouth of the canyon—

Mundo's heart lurched as he heard a horse lunge wildly in deep water.

"What's that?" he heard a rustler call. "What's wrong with the stock?"

And just that fast, the outlaws were wide awake and running.

More loud splashing noises came from the spring. Was it possible that the girl was still down at the water, he wondered, clumsily scaring the horses? Had she even caught Riley's buckskin gelding? If the outlaws all headed down to the spring and busied themselves with the Navajo, Mundo might yet manage to escape before they realized he was gone.

He dug his spurs into the sorrel's flanks, desperately urging it to run. In the dark, the horse was hesitant to go so fast, and normally, so was Mundo. But he had no choices now. He leaned almost flat against the sorrel's neck, hoping he recalled exactly the best way to reach the narrow canyon's opening.

Yes! There was a vague sense of light, an openness,

between the rocks and scraggly pines. He squeezed the sorrel harder with his knees and thighs. He was going to make it!

And then, without warning, a man loomed up in the path before him. He reached out toward Mundo, but he didn't fire a gun. It was Private Riley.

He stood, half-bent over, his face filled with pain. He had sworn to warn the outlaws if Mundo or the Navajo tried to leave without him. But they knew about the planned escape now. Mundo knew there was nothing Riley could do to stop him.

But he couldn't just ride by and leave him there. Barely slowing down, he leaned over to grab Riley's out-stretched hand. When he did this with Chayito, her hand wrapped around *his* wrist, and their grips were tightly locked.

But Riley's grasp was limp, and he did not jump high enough to reach the sorrel. He pitched over and fell on the ground.

By now Mundo could hear men on horseback heading toward him. A gunshot rang out near the spring. He *had* to get out of the canyon! He could not waste another second!

Still, instinctively he circled back toward Riley, who was struggling to get back on his feet. He couldn't risk another missed pass. He knew Riley lacked the strength to swing himself up on the horse.

But there was almost nothing Mundo could not do on one. Without thinking, he jerked the sorrel to a stop, clinging to its mane as he leaped off. With the other hand he dragged Riley to his feet and half-pushed, half-threw him over the horse's back. Mundo jumped up behind him in the darkness and pummeled the sorrel with both spurs.

The startled animal bolted out of the mouth of the canyon with yelling cowboys only thirty yards away. Mundo urged the horse to gallop down the cliff, faster and faster, ignoring the flying bullets and the risk of night riding at such speed. He clung to Riley's shirt with one hand and the sorrel's mane with the other. He knew that the awkward burden of carrying two men, one of them lying on his stomach, greatly slowed the sorrel down.

As Mundo heard a horse gallop out of the dense scrub to his right, he leaned to the left, certain he could expect a bullet momentarily. But the sounds of the cowboys remained some distance behind him, even though the other horse caught up.

He caught a glimpse of the buckskin as it roared up beside him, then pressed ahead. The Navajo girl fiercely gripped her saddle horn as she bounced up and down. Still, she kept on going and never tried to slow her mount. Heedless of prairie dog holes and piles of broken shale, the two horses fled across a wild land shielded by the wind-danced darkness.

After an hour or more, Mundo finally felt the ground start to even out beneath him. He realized that they had reached the desert and the heart of the dust storm. He could no longer hear hoofbeats behind him. No yelling. No gunshots now. The rustlers seemed to have given up the chase.

Still, he kept the sorrel running until he realized

that Riley's body was slipping from his grasp. Mundo's fingers were fatigued and cramped from clinging so hard to the bloody jacket, to Riley's shoulder, to the sorrel's flying mane. Bit by bit Riley shifted downward until Mundo could not stop him from sliding to the ground.

Chapter Ten

A̲t first, Tenchi did not realize that Riley had fallen from Mundo's horse. She was having enough trouble fending off the gale-force dust storm and trying to control the buckskin. But once she realized that she was riding alone, she turned back to see if the Hispanic boy had left her. She found him dismounted and struggling to pick up Private Riley.

"Help me!" the rich kid hollered into the wind. "We've got to get him back up!"

"Is there any way you can tie him on? The horses are crazy!" she shouted, wondering how the injured boy had made it this far. "We've got to find shelter!"

"You're the one who said you could handle a dust storm! 'I am a *Navajo!*'" he mimicked.

She wasn't about to explain that she'd been a captive so long that much of her childhood training now seemed like make-believe stories to her. She knew that her father had once escaped a group of enemy warriors by riding into a horrific dust storm, but she no longer remembered the details.

"*I'm* not the problem!" she yelled. "The Texan can't go on!"

He mumbled something which Tenchi guessed meant "the Texan's probably dead." But she wasn't certain. All she was sure of was that the three of them had escaped from the outlaws, which more or less put them on the same side.

"I think we should just stop here," she decided. "Let's try to get him comfortable. They can't find us in the dark even if they're still looking."

That much was true. Tenchi had no idea where they were, which direction they had run. Surely the bandits, who'd broken off the chase long ago, didn't either. Not even a trained Navajo tracker could follow hoofprints at night in a dust storm. How could Texan rustlers?

"All right!" the Hispanic boy agreed. "Take your *rebozo* and cover his face tightly. Then cover him with the blanket. If he keeps breathing in that flying dirt while he's unconscious, he'll suffocate."

Tenchi wasn't sure he could see her when she nodded.

"Wrap the wound up, too, or it'll get infected. We don't have any water to wash out the sand."

"There's nothing to wrap it with!" she called back.

"Use your sash!"

"It's woolen. It'll stick to the wound."

"Your skirt is soft! Use that!" he ordered. "Do what you have to do."

He took hold of Tenchi's bridle and waited impatiently for her to dismount. For a second she thought he might actually pull her off.

Instead, he leaped back on his own unsaddled mount and tugged on the buckskin's reins. Tenchi crisply pulled them away from him.

He was leaving her! He was abandoning Private Riley. So much for thinking the three of them were in this mess together!

"If you don't have the decency to stay here and help, at least leave us a horse!" she barked. "You don't need two!"

With an exasperated look, the rich boy released the reins. "If I don't find a place to hobble the horses, we won't have either one in the morning," he irritably explained. "I don't know how far I'll have to go to do that, but I'll bring them back at sunup. Then we'll all head back to my ranch. It shouldn't take more than a day."

Tenchi shook her head. "I've got no reason to trust you. Without a horse, I'll die out here!" She knew that every kind of predator stalked this harsh country— cougars, bears, bobcats. Even the snakes and scorpions were poisonous. It was surely miles and miles to any source of water, food, or medical help. And the outlaws had horses—lots of them. When the storm stopped and daylight came, they could just look out across the flat land and *see* Tenchi and Riley.

Tenchi didn't really think they'd come for either one of them. But if the Hispanic boy was telling the truth, he was worth a fortune. Add that to an outlaw's pride, and Kurtzer just might send Toland after *him*.

~~~

It took Mundo several minutes to convince the Navajo that he should take the horses. He didn't think she really believed he'd come back, but at least she realized that there was no way she could keep an unprotected horse from bolting in this kind of dust storm. He wasn't entirely sure he could do it himself, but he might have a chance if he could find decent shelter.

But the desert didn't have many dense clumps of high shrubs or trees, and Mundo couldn't see much in the dark. The storm was unrelenting, and several times in the next two hours the horses panicked. Struggling to keep them under control, he finally gave up when he found a lone ironwood surrounded by a thick patch of saltbrush that would partially break the force of the wind. It wasn't what he'd hoped for, but he and the horses were utterly spent. Mundo knew he wasn't likely to find anything better tonight.

He found a picket pin by touch in Riley's saddle-bags, but he could only use it for one horse. He chose the sorrel. He used the buckskin's reins to tie it securely to a branch and pulled off the saddle to use as a windbreak for his own head.

As he settled down with his back to the storm, Mundo pulled his shirt up over his eyes and curled into a ball. The stinging sand still whipped his arms and legs.

For the first time in hours he had time to think about all that had happened since he'd left the Roadrunner yesterday. It seemed like a week ago! He was exhausted, frightened, and sporting an egg-sized lump on his head where Riley had slugged him with his carbine. Worse yet, Mundo knew his troubles were not over.

He was still a long way from home and somehow had picked up the burden of two helpless strangers. In the canyon, he had been driven by his own desperation, but once he'd lost the outlaws, he realized that both the Texan and the Navajo would need his help to survive. Even though they were his traditional enemies, it just wouldn't be right to abandon them.

But neither could he spend much time nursemaiding them, because he *had* to rush back to the ranch. The outlaws didn't have to know where Mundo was to demand a ransom from Julio. Nor would it take long for them to realize, once they scouted out the Roadrunner, that there were very few men left there to protect the women or the stock.

He tried not to think about his father, and where he might be tonight. He didn't even know if *Papá* was still alive! How ashamed he would be if he knew about Mundo's pathetic showing in his first battle.

Next time, Mundo vowed, *I will fight like a real soldier. And if I am ever captured again, it will not be with a Texan and a Navajo, but with my own kind.*

Chapter Eleven

It was the dream that woke Riley up, a dream that he was being suffocated in a huge dune of shifting sand.

He struggled to the surface—of the sand and the dream—and found himself fighting some sort of shawl and the solid slab of a woven wool blanket. With a gasp as his panic met full consciousness, he thrust it aside.

It was daylight. He was alive.

It took a moment for him to wrestle with those two facts, to be sure they went together. Another pile of realizations tumbled end over end.

He was alone.

He had been shot but not killed.

The rich boy had saved him from the bandits.

Riley pulled the last trio of thoughts together before he realized what all the facts meant wrapped up together.

Rivera dumped me here to die.

He closed his itching eyes for a moment, telling himself it was sand he briskly wiped away, not tears. There was never a good time for a soldier to cry, even when he was abandoned. Even when his best friend died. Even when the sergeant ordered him to keep on shooting, to waste no time on grief for Joey....

He fought back the tears and the memories. He knew he had to concentrate. His survival would depend on everything he did from this moment on. He could not afford a single error if he wanted to stay alive.

Riley looked around for his horse and his soldier's gear. There was nothing. Had Rivera taken everything? His buckskin ... his canteen ... and his carbine. A soldier's gun is *everything*, he'd been taught again and again. He'd practiced for a million hours, it seemed, and there was nothing he couldn't hit when he had to. He'd had the same weapon since he left Texas. He and Joey had both lucked out and been given recent-model carbines. But Joey's had jammed when he needed it most, and ...

Riley couldn't finish the thought. He couldn't waste time bemoaning things he couldn't change. At least he had the blanket, although how he did Riley could not explain, since the girl had been wearing it before she'd left him in the canyon.

He pondered the thought, staring at the blue-and-red blanket. It was the same one. He was *sure* she had taken it with her. That meant the Rivera boy had followed her, or she had followed him, and the blanket had fallen off right over Riley....

Which was impossible.

He looked at the weave again, vaguely aware of the complex, perfect pattern, pondering the fact that it had covered his face completely. So had the shawl. It had practically been *wrapped* around his head.

Somebody had covered up his mouth and nose to protect him from the dust storm.

He took a deep breath. Maybe he had not been deserted. At least he had not been dumped off the horse to die.

Maybe ...

Groggily he struggled to sit upright, to cast a thoughtful eye across the empty land. It was bleak and bare. The sky—now that the wind eased up some—was a magnificent shade of blue. It reminded him of the ocean. No matter how far he went, there was more ahead, and just as much behind him. On the desert or the open sea, he never felt hemmed in.

Maybe, thought Riley, *the sky just looks beautiful because I am alive to see it*. Between the sand and the cactus and the grim-faced circling vultures, the land *was* pretty plain.

Then he saw the girl, the Navajo, heading toward him. At first he thought it must be a mirage caused by his desperate need for help. He wasn't sure what she could do for him, but she was a human being he vaguely knew. Somehow it made his chances for survival a whole lot better than they'd been a moment before.

But that didn't explain what she was doing here. He distinctly remembered that when she'd slipped off toward the spring, he'd been certain she would not come back for him. He hadn't trusted Rivera either, and he suspected that if he hadn't been waiting in the mouth of the canyon, the other boy would not have bothered to rescue him.

Riley noticed that the Indian's eyes were bloodshot and she was covered with dirt. She wore neither sash nor *rebozo*. For some reason that he could not understand, she had deep, ragged tears along the hem of her yellow skirt. Of course it still covered most of her limbs, but Riley had never seen a female's bare knees before and he knew it wasn't proper for him to do so now. Even if she *was* an Indian, she was still a girl.

She did not speak until she reached him. "You lived through the night," she said without much expression.

"I guess." He waited for her to explain it.

"You still look very weak."

He nodded. He was already exhausted from sitting up.

"How's the wound?"

"Probably full of dirt."

The girl shook her head. "No, I wrapped it up very tightly. Not too much should have slipped in."

Touched and startled, Riley pulled the blanket completely off his chest. He tugged open the shirt of his long johns to look at the wound. All he could see was a pink sash and ripped, blood-caked yellow cotton strips, red where the blood had soaked through.

"You, uh, did a good job." She said nothing, so Riley pursued the conversation. "Do you have a name?"

She glared at him. "Even Indian slaves have names. They have to call us something, and numbers would be awkward."

Riley took a deep breath. Talking to this girl was not going to be easy. But what could he expect?

"So what do they call you? What should I call you?"

For a moment she glanced away. "*They* call me Tenchi."

"You have another name?"

She turned terrible eyes on him, the eyes of a prisoner of war. Angrily she drew her hand into a fist and tapped her chest. "It is a secret name, known only to my people. I do not tell my captors what it is, but I will never forget it."

Riley didn't know where to go with that. He was getting woozy again. He had to stretch back out on the sand. He'd been on his back all night, though, so now he rolled clumsily to his side.

"What happened to my buckskin?" he tried again, wishing she would just tell him what had happened. He didn't have the strength to keep pulling out information fact by fact.

"The other boy took it. He said he had to find shelter for the horses."

Riley's blue eyes widened. "And you believed that?"

Tenchi glowered at him. "No, but I couldn't stop him. Besides, you had already fallen off. If one of us had not stayed to keep your lungs from filling up with dust while you were unconscious, you would have died in the night."

Now Riley was really stuck. The Navajo girl had saved his life, but she wasn't very happy about it. The Rivera boy had snookered them both. If he and Riley hadn't threatened to reveal her plan to the bandits, she would have been safe by now.

"Well, I'm alive." *Just barely,* he could have added. But he wasn't sure whether it was better or worse to let her know how very helpless he was. She'd only earned a tiny grain of his trust.

The girl was still standing uncertainly beside him. "You won't be much longer if I can't find some water. There's nothing nearby. I've looked and looked—"

"He didn't leave the canteen? It was almost full."

She shook her head.

"And my carbine? Was it still on the horse?"

"Yes." She lifted one shoulder toward the west, where, at a distance, a hint of plant life was barely visible. "He took that, too."

Riley closed his eyes. Texas had never seemed so far away from him. His wound throbbed unbearably. He didn't think he could get up.

"My people have ways of surviving in the desert," Tenchi said, holding up her knife. "There is a kind of cactus they will eat, big and full, that sort of takes the place of water."

She demonstrated how she could use the knife to peel off the spines of the cactus.

If she found one.

"Do they grow around here?"

To his surprise, Tenchi shrugged. "I have no idea. I have never lived this far south. I do know it has not been a good year."

That's for sure, he wanted to mumble. But then he realized she was not talking about the war. She was talking about the cactus.

"What do you mean?"

"There's been no rain to speak of in Santa Fe for longer than I can remember. I would have heard if there had been much down here."

Riley mentally filled in the rest of the picture. No rain, no water holes. No rain, shrunken cactus.

It didn't matter. He had no strength to move. Even if the girl found water somewhere, how would she carry it to him?

"I did not escape the rustlers to sit here and watch you die," Tenchi announced a little bluntly. "I am going to find water, or something that is moist and juicy inside. When I do, I will bring you some."

Riley nodded.

"If the rich boy comes back, you tell him I headed that way." She pointed east.

Riley followed her finger with his eyes. He could see no sign of moisture, no trees, no clumps of cactus. "Why that way?"

She shook out the tiny pockets of sand that had collected in the gathers of her torn skirt. "Because he went the other way. There is no point in covering ground in the same direction."

She swallowed hard, and for just a moment, Riley saw through the window of her well-hidden pain. She didn't believe the Rivera kid would come back with rested mounts and water any more than he did.

Chapter Twelve

Mundo slept till the sun was high. When he opened his eyes, it took him a few moments to remember where he was, and why. He was covered with grit and his head was throbbing. His thirst was intense, but he only allowed himself a single swallow from Riley's canteen. He was desert-trained and knew he'd have to ration every drop. Slowly he dragged himself to his feet and gazed at the land around him. Mundo was a long way south of the Roadrunner, and the land here was not as rich. It was mainly barren and utterly dry, but here and there he saw a lone paloverde or a cluster of cholla. Off in the distance, he could see a pile of broken shale and one small butte rising. He saw no sign of water.

He saw no sign of the sorrel, either, which had apparently escaped in the night. It had probably panicked again.

The buckskin neighed a greeting, though, tossing its head impatiently. Mundo knew the horse was hungry and thirsty, too, but there wasn't a lot he could do about it. He filled his hand with just enough water to moisten the poor beast's mouth and spoke to it kindly. He'd make sure it was fed the finest Roadrunner grain when he got home.

Wearily he saddled up and started back toward the place he thought he'd left the Indian girl and Private Riley. After his long night ride in the storm, his memory of the land was poor, and he wasn't entirely sure he was heading in the right direction until he spied a pair of red-headed vultures about mid-day. It wasn't hard to guess they were circling Riley.

When he first spotted the Texan lying flat in the sand, Mundo thought he'd come too late. He felt sad, in a curious sort of way, but also, to his shame, a bit relieved. He'd done his duty. Now he could get on his way.

He eased Riley's buckskin to a stop and slowly dismounted, holding onto the reins with one hand and Riley's carbine with the other. Riley lay on his back, utterly still, clutching the Indian blanket like a child.

There was no sign of the Navajo.

"I'm sorry you didn't make it, Texan," Mundo murmured. "I should have known that Indian would leave you to die."

To his surprise, Riley's eyelids fluttered open. "You!" he said. "You've got my horse. And my gun."

Mundo jerked back a step. "Well, of course, 'me.' Who did you expect to find out here?"

Riley managed to sit up, but he still looked awfully feeble.

"The outlaws, maybe. Headin' for the Staked Plains

or lookin' for you." Despite the gruffness of his tone, Riley's dirty face could not hide his great relief.

"They wouldn't be looking for me if you hadn't blabbered everything you knew about me."

"True 'nuff. If I hadn't told 'em, they would've killed you outright."

Mundo didn't answer. He knew Riley had saved his life. He wasn't sure that made him worthy of any gratitude, considering how things had turned out. He wasn't even sure if Riley had done it on purpose, or just blurted out the information about the Riveras' wealth to make himself look more important. Before that, the other Texans certainly hadn't paid any attention to the fact that he'd gotten shot and captured a New Mexican.

Mundo handed Riley the canteen. "Just take a little," he cautioned. "We've got to make it last."

Riley stood up shakily and took a long swallow. He fondly patted his horse. Then his blue eyes squinted. "By the way, Rich Boy," he drawled suspiciously, "how come it is that yesterday you couldn't talk nothin' but Spanish and now you're talkin' English like a house afire?"

"You convinced yourself right off that I could only speak one language. I didn't see any good reason to change your mind. I thought I might learn something."

"So what did you learn?"

"I learned that we better call a temporary truce until we reach my people," Mundo admitted reluctantly. His eyes met Riley's. "You can stop calling me Rich Boy. Everybody calls me Mundo. Do you think you can ride?"

Riley heaved a mighty sigh. "What's my other choice? Lay here till the vultures pluck out my eyeballs?"

"Pretty much," Mundo answered. "I can send back help when I reach the ranch, but to tell you the truth, I don't know how long that'll take."

Riley grunted something incomprehensible.

"Get on your feet, then." Mundo knew he wasn't sounding very kind, but he'd been through too much himself to feel much sympathy toward a Texan. After all, Riley wouldn't be in this predicament if his army hadn't invaded New Mexico.

"I'll try to ride upright this time," Riley murmured as Mundo slung the carbine over his shoulder and cupped his hands for the other boy's boot. As he boosted Riley up, the other boy half-stretched, half-fell across the high-horned saddle. Mundo had to clutch the reins and push Riley into place all at the same time. Then he grabbed the blanket and swept up behind the Texan with the grace of one born to ride. He'd always heard that Texans were devils on horseback. He wondered how Riley rode when he was more than half-alive.

Mundo checked the sun, which was straight up noon, and learned nothing. He'd come from the west, more or less, so he turned to the left and hoped that once the sun began to sink it would confirm he'd headed in the right direction.

Abruptly Riley said, "The girl went east."

"What?" Mundo had long since dismissed the girl. She was a Navajo, and she'd obviously left Riley to die out here. He didn't think she was even worth mentioning.

"I said, the girl went east. Tenchi, her name is. She said to tell you."

"East?" he repeated, perplexed that she'd left a message for him. It had never even crossed his mind that she had a name. "She said to tell *me*?"

"She said you'd gone in the other direction, so she'd cover new ground. She said there was no point in lookin' for water in the same place."

Mundo shook his head and clucked the buckskin into a slow, steady jog. So the girl had waited until morning. Even left the blanket with Riley. That surprised him. Of course, last night he'd really believed, for a moment there, that she would follow his orders and stay with the injured boy. He was a Rivera. He was used to having people obey.

But now he remembered clearly how she'd vowed that nothing would block her path to freedom. *What else,* he thought grimly, *should I have expected from a Navajo?*

"Don't you think we ought to, uh, try to find her or leave her a message?" Riley asked.

Mundo didn't bother to reply.

Chapter Thirteen

It did not take Tenchi long to realize that she was in over her head. She had longed for freedom since she had first been captured as a child, but she was no longer prepared for it. She had known more about life in the desert as an eight-year-old.

Since then her home had been Santa Fe. When she'd first arrived in the city, the constant noise had terrified her. To her surprise, she missed it now. Santa Fe was such a lively place, always full of braying mule teams, grunting oxen, lumbering wagons, colorful characters, and laughing children that brightened up her days.

And she had not been the only slave. Others of her race were held captive there, and though Tenchi could only see them rarely, it was a comfort to know she was not the only Navajo. Of course, it was not the same as living with her close-knit band. Some of the other Navajo slaves had been captives for so long that they barely remembered their lives as free people. They had long since given up any hope of going home.

"I have lived with my owner since I was a baby," an old Navajo had once told Tenchi. "I know no other life. This is my family now."

Tenchi might have felt the same way if she had been "adopted" in the way some of the very young Navajo captives had. But since she'd been bounced around and mistreated more often than she'd been given the respect one human owes another, she had never been able to forget her dream.

But in her vision of escape, she survived on the land as her tribe had always done. In her memory, Navajo country was filled with opportunities for good food and sweet water. But here, so far to the south, she found nothing, absolutely nothing, that looked edible. Tenchi knew that her mother would have known what plants to pick, which needed to be cooked, which were poisonous to humans. Her father would have known how to kill small creatures, or even large ones, with only a knife. And anyone who had grown up with the tribe would have known how to travel back to her people.

But Tenchi had no idea where she was, or how to return to Santa Fe, let alone to Navajo country. She had carefully taken note of her trail since she'd left Private Riley, and she was reasonably sure she could get back to him. But what good would that do either of them? He couldn't help her, and if she didn't find something to eat or drink soon, it would be too late for her to help him.

She considered the possibility that the rich boy would return. She thought it was unlikely. But if he did come, and Riley was dead or unconscious, he would not know how to find her even if he wanted to.

And she didn't think tracking her down would be very high on his list of concerns.

He reminded her of the son of an owner she had once belonged to. The man had three children, one Tenchi's age and two younger. The oldest one had been cocky, like the Rivera boy, and went out of his way to torment her. But the younger two, one girl and one boy, had attached themselves to Tenchi and loved her as though she were their big sister. The boy tattled on his big brother whenever he was cruel, and the girl secretly taught Tenchi how to read. Best of all, they had made her feel special.

She had learned to care deeply for those two little children. During the years she spent with them, she had stopped waiting for the warriors, stopped trying to escape. She had settled in, deciding to make the best of it. Then their father had made a disastrous mining investment and lost everything he had. The children had wailed and begged him not to sell Tenchi to a rich old man who was cold as ice, but he had needed the cash to buy food.

Tenchi needed food now. In Santa Fe, she would have known how to find it—buy it, make it, steal it if she had to. But out of the city she was helpless.

She had forgotten how to be a Navajo. And out here it did no good that she had learned how to live as a slave.

They rode for days, it seemed to Riley. The two of them fit poorly on the horse together, even though Mundo let Riley take the saddle while he hung on behind. It embarrassed Riley that the other boy had to keep one arm around him, holding him on, but he knew that if Mundo let go for a second he'd tumble right off.

The wound was bleeding again. It hurt hideously. Riley was dizzy half the time, and always groggy.

Still, he dared not complain, any more than he'd risked complaining to the outlaws. Riley knew that he'd been lucky, incredibly lucky, so far. Mundo was trying to help him, but with great and obvious reluctance. He didn't dare cause any more problems for him.

They stopped to rest only once, when Mundo claimed the buckskin was fatigued. So was Riley. He collapsed as soon as Mundo helped him dismount. Soon after, he fell asleep—as he had several times in the saddle—and it seemed to Riley that the sun had shifted considerably when Mundo roused him and helped him back on the horse.

"So how long have you been in the army?" Mundo asked after they'd ridden a long time in awkward silence.

"Not too long. Just since the war began."

"You mean since the Texans invaded New Mexico?"

"I mean since the Union declared war on the Confederacy."

Mundo grunted. "This war—the North and South—has nothing to do with us. We just want to be left alone."

"You got Yankee soldiers all over this territory. They got to be drummed out."

"We tried that once, when we still belonged to Mexico. It can't be done."

"It *will* be done," insisted Riley. "Nobody from up North is gonna tell Texas soldiers what to do."

"My *papá* says that the North just wants the South to stop keeping slaves."

Riley had an answer for that. "The really poor folks up North ain't treated no better than black slaves in Texas. And I done heard that you got starvin' Hispanics on the big ranches in New Mexico that are just slaves called by another name."

"That's not true!" Mundo's voice grew dark. "Our cowboys and servants are practically family. The Roadrunner is their home! They don't want to live anywhere else."

"But could they leave it, if they wanted to?"

"Of course, they could! If they paid my father what they owe him."

"Ah."

"He is very good to them. Takes care of all their problems. Loans them money whenever they have need of it."

"So they're always in debt to him? They can never really pay him off?"

Mundo expelled a harsh breath. "It is not like Texas slavery," he insisted.

Riley shook his head. "What about the Injuns? Don't some of y'all work them as slaves?"

"They are not slaves either! The Navajos are *prisoners of war*. They steal our livestock, attack our men, and take our women and children. What do you do in Texas when Indians take your loved ones?"

"We kill 'em. If we can." Riley realized they had finally found some common ground.

"So we are not so different, then." The anger in Mundo's voice subsided. After a moment, he asked, "Why did you try to save that Indian girl? Didn't you know she was a Navajo?"

Riley shrugged uncomfortably. "She was a girl in trouble. I didn't see her do no wrong."

They both fell silent after that. Hours later, when dusk started creeping across the desert, Riley began to hope that Mundo would decide to stop. But they had come upon nothing that looked like shelter. They'd eaten a few brick-hard biscuits from his saddlebags and shared half a canteenful of water. Mundo wouldn't let Riley drink all he wanted. Riley suspected he was holding it back for himself.

"We gonna keep on ridin' till sunup?" he finally asked.

"If that's what it takes."

"You ain't gonna find no help in the darkness. My horse is likely to break a leg. Then where would we be?"

"We ought to be closer to home by now." Mundo's voice was tense. "We've headed due north all day. I just didn't ride that far before the battle, or even afterwards. We ought to reach the Roadrunner's south grazing lands any time."

"Is there help there?" Riley asked. "Ranch house? Line shack?"

Mundo sighed. "No, but I'd sleep better on my land, or even on a neighbor's. At least I'd know we could make it home tomorrow." His voice dropped as he mumbled. "We've got to get there on time."

"On time for what?" Riley groused. "Before I die?"

"You telling me you need to rest?" Mundo asked sharply.

By now it was nearly dark. At least, with the wind heavy with dirt, it seemed to be.

"What do you think, Rich Boy? I'm half-dead and I've been in the saddle all day. Do you—"

"Call me Mundo."

Before Riley could answer, a tremendous cloud of dust—like living soil—rushed at his face. He ducked, then burst out loud when the cloud swerved to avoid him, "What was that?"

"Bats!" Mundo burst out almost joyfully. "The bats are coming out!"

Riley couldn't imagine why Mundo sounded so excited. Was it possible he was afraid?

He could see them clearly now—not one or two but a stream of them, pouring over the bone-dry land.

"Riley, we're saved!"

Riley half twisted in the saddle to see Mundo's face. The effort nearly killed him.

"Are you nuts? Unless you're going to shoot one for dinner or try to drink their blood—"

"Don't you get it?" The buckskin bolted forward as Mundo dug in his spurs. "Bats don't live loose in the desert! They have to have shelter. Where there's a bat, Riley, there's got to be a house or a barn or a cave."

Chapter Fourteen

The bats, as it turned out, were flying out of an old Indian village, which had been abandoned and long since decayed. Still, Mundo was right about one thing. The bats had found a desert shelter, and the boys could share it with them.

Riley had heard of earthquakes in this part of the country, and it looked as though nature had done a pretty good job of shaking down the huge flat rocks that had once formed the village houses. Only a few sagging walls remained, leaning toward each other like cattle in a bad storm. Riley could even tell, when he got close enough, that enormously long stones had been put in place here and there to form doorway tops and bottoms. There were no roofs, but he could tell there once had been.

Mundo circled the village before he headed back toward the heaviest concentration of stones at the intersection of two crumbling walls. "This looks like the best spot to hide from the wind," he declared as he helped Riley dismount again.

Riley vowed not to fall on his face this time, but he was so light-headed that his legs gave out under him. Mundo half-carried, half-dragged him to the corner of the ruins. More bats fluttered out. The ground beneath Riley was rich with dried guano.

"You'll get used to it," said Mundo. "Bats are delicate creatures. If they can survive in these ruins, so can we."

Riley felt himself tense as Mundo led the horse out into a clump of thick grasses. *Don't leave me,* he wanted to beg him. If Mundo rode off, this shelter would only buy him a day or two. A little protection from the night cold and endless wind. But he still had no food or water. Unless he got well enough to walk—

"I'm going to build a fire. Get you warm. At least you've got the blanket."

Riley closed his eyes in relief. Mundo was back.

After he nursed some dried weeds and dead cactus parts into friendly flames, Mundo hunkered down before the fire and closed his eyes. Riley realized, for the first time, that Mundo was feeling beat, too. He'd been through a lot since yesterday, and he'd been pushing hard.

"What's the big hurry to reach your ranch?" he asked cautiously. "It seems to me if you can get help somewhere closer—"

"I'm not worried about help for *me,*" Mundo stated briskly. "I must get word of the outlaws to my brother and sister."

"To stop them from giving away the money?"

"To warn them to defend their lives!" Mundo's voice sounded squeaky. "You know that Kurtzer ordered

Toland to kill us last night. You know that he will do anything for money. He will go to the Roadrunner, or send someone. He will tell them that he holds me hostage, that he will kill me if they don't give him everything. I must get there first, to prove I am safe." His voice dropped to a near-whisper. "And to keep Julio from going to our bank in Santa Fe to get the money."

Riley felt stupid, but he just didn't get it. He was too groggy to think. "Why is that so important? As long as you get there before they've actually exchanged the cash?"

"Forget the cash! Julio can't leave the ranch! The rustlers would kill him the instant they found him alone with the money." Mundo's voice rose sharply. "And even if they didn't, we have no men at the Roadrunner to spare. They have all gone off to fight the Texans! There are not enough left to defend my sister. To defend the others! To defend our land. Kurtzer's group is the worst of the Texans, the animals who came and slaughtered my—"

"Whoa," Riley barked. "Stop right there. I may be feelin' lower'n a snake's hips, but I ain't dead. I ain't gonna let you talk like that about my people."

"You are proud to come from the same place as the outlaws who tried to kill you last night?" Mundo asked.

"Of course not. They're killers and thieves. Killers and thieves come from everywhere. But you act like all Texans are just like them. Most of us are farmers, merchants, cowboys . . . even fishermen. Mundo, we're just ordinary people."

"People who invade the land of those who did you no harm. People who use land-lust to wage war!"

"I ain't here to get no land," Riley shot back, struggling against his fresh dizziness. "I'm here to save the South from the Yankees. I don't cotton much to slavery, but that don't mean I'll let some uppity abolitionist Northerners tell good ol' Texas boys what to do! If New Mexico hadn't gone with the North, I wouldn't be here fightin' you!"

"Sure you would!" Mundo snapped. "There is always some reason for Texans to steal our stock and our best growing land. My father has fought them again and again. And this time, he has probably died at the hands of your monster-men!"

Riley leaned up on one elbow. He stared at Mundo. "Your daddy fought our troops?"

Mundo nodded. His eyelids grew red. "Yesterday."

"That's when you ran into me. You were looking for him?"

There was a long silence, so long Riley felt the need to fill it, but he couldn't think of anything to say.

"I wanted to fight Texans with my father," Mundo finally confessed, "but he did not care. He went wild when your soldiers shot our foreman. He charged into battle and I ... I lost sight of him."

It was dark by the time Tenchi approached the old Indian village, creeping toward the half-hidden campfire. It had taken her a long time to find something to take back to Riley, only to discover he was gone.

Fortunately the dust had died down enough to leave the hoofprints of one horse in the sand. She'd followed them all day until she'd spotted the bats, and then the flames. It was long past midnight, and she was exhausted. She was reasonably certain that the two boys were camping out in the ruins, but she could take no chances. The outlaws could be anywhere.

She froze when she heard a hammer cock. Apparently she wasn't as quiet as she should have been.

"It's Tenchi," she said quickly. "I brought something for you." She waited in the darkness, listening to her heart pound.

"How'd you sneak up on us like that?" It was the Texan's weary drawl.

Tenchi was surprised he was even conscious. It took her a moment to realize that he, not the rich boy, held the carbine.

"Navajos are born sneaky," the New Mexican said. "Though she's the first one I ever met who had trouble stealing a horse."

Tenchi took a quiet breath as she heard Riley set the carbine down.

"What you got there?" he asked.

"Part of a fishhook barrel cactus. Not water, but it will ease your thirst." She came close enough to see the boys' faces by the fire. Riley looked terrible, far closer to death. The Hispanic boy looked wary.

"Give it to him," he said.

"I have to cut off the spines."

He glared at her. "You've had all day to do that!"

"It would have rotted if I had! Don't you think it would have been easier than wrestling with these spines in my ripped-up skirt?"

The boys couldn't see her clothes in the dark, but they knew that between the bandage strips she'd torn for Riley and the daylong battle with the cactus, they were in shreds.

The angry silence filled the night. A poor-will whooped several times. Then Riley said a single, tired word to Tenchi.

"Thanks."

It hung there, untouched and untouchable by any of them. It was the word that none of them had uttered since their escape.

"Thanks to you, too, Mundo," Private Riley admitted slowly. "Thanks for coming back."

They sat in silence as the darkness softened the hard words they'd exchanged. Somewhere to the east, a pack of coyotes began their pre-hunt howl. Instinctively the three of them edged a little closer to the fire.

Without speaking, Tenchi started cutting off the spines of the cactus and handed raw, dripping pieces to both boys. They scarfed them down like hungry wolves. Tenchi saved one more piece for herself.

She didn't know whether or not the boys could tell that she'd learned, in her one lone day on the desert, that she could not survive out here alone. Even if they didn't want her to join them, she needed to share their campfire, to diminish her fears, to hear the sound of a human voice. She needed Riley's wry courage and Mundo's cocky confidence that he could lead them to his home.

When they finished eating, nobody talked for a while. Mundo offered Tenchi a little water, then gave some to Riley. He did not, she noticed, drink any of the last few precious drops himself.

"So what're we gonna do now?" Riley asked.

It hurt Tenchi to listen to him. His breathing was slow and awkward. His lazy drawl could not conceal the terrible pain his wound caused him.

"Now that we've found shelter, and somethin' to eat and drink—"

"We haven't found a *source*," Mundo cut him off. "All we've found is shelter. Primitive, but enough to keep you a little warmer, Riley, and enough to stop the wind from blowing out a nighttime fire. But there's no stream here, or seep or well. And I don't have time to hunt, even if I could find a jackrabbit or a pronghorn." Without saying her name, he asked Tenchi, "I don't suppose you can kill game like a real Navajo?"

She swallowed her resentment. It wasn't her fault she hadn't learned all the ways of her tribe! It was the fault of people of his race—and the Texan's.

"Navajo warriors do the hunting," she informed him harshly. "I learned to weave."

Riley pulled the blanket up around his chin. "This one of yours?" he asked.

She nodded.

"It's warm. Full of blood and dirt by now, I'm afraid, but ... toasty."

He smiled at her. She managed to smile back.

"So, we're still working with one horse, one almost-empty canteen, one knife, and one carbine," Mundo continued. "I've got to head north. The question is whether or not to drag you two along or have you wait here until I can send somebody back."

Tenchi watched as Riley closed his eyes. She wasn't sure which seemed more awful to him—being left again or having to put up with Mundo. The Hispanic boy was all too good at giving orders.

"How much wood is here?" she asked.

"For a fire this small? Maybe three nights," answered Mundo. "The wind has just sort of blown it against the walls. You can pick it up when it's daylight."

Tenchi nodded.

"You think you can find more food?"

"I can try. I saw some clumps of prickly pear cactus, but I guess it's too early for fruit. I'm not sure—"

"Tomorrow you could look some more."

Her eyes met his coldly. Tenchi knew he was only trying to convince himself that she and Riley could survive if he left them there. It didn't matter what she said. He would go anyway.

Chapter Fifteen

When Mundo woke up in the morning, the wind was blowing harder. It never stopped for long, but sometimes it was worse than others. He knew it would be another endless day.

He sat up, brushed off the worst of the dirt from his face, and glanced across the dead campfire. Riley was asleep, his chest barely moving. Sometime during the night he had pushed off the blanket. One end had caught a few sparks from the fire.

The girl was awake. With blank eyes she stared at Mundo. She said nothing and he didn't want her to.

He stood up, instinctively glancing around for something to eat or drink, and forced himself to face the fact that there was nothing. He'd given the last of the water to Riley's horse last night. Without a lot more soon, the buckskin couldn't take him much farther.

Avoiding the girl's cold gaze, Mundo picked up the saddle he'd used as a pillow and lugged it over to the tethered horse. The buckskin nuzzled him roughly, as though in search of food or drink. Its bit was green and slimy from eating scrawny clumps of burrobrush. Mundo felt guilty for leaving the bridle on all night, but he didn't dare take any chances. He'd tied the reins to a half-dead paloverde tree and crudely hobbled the horse with its saddle cinch.

In the pale daylight, he could see a few small buttes to the east, but no sign of any draw or stream. The cactus wrens were already calling *chug-chug-chug* as he saddled up. Other than that, the desert was silent. It wasn't hard for him to hear the girl's footsteps as she crept up behind him.

"You're just going to leave him here?"

Mundo did not answer.

"He'll probably die without help. There's nothing I can do but ... give him false hope."

Mundo tugged on the cinch. "That's about all I can do for him, either. There's a lot more I can do for my family."

"Is that what this is about?" Kindness laced her stern Navajo voice. "Your family is in trouble?"

He turned to her briskly. "Riley told the outlaws that I was worth a fortune. My brother will do anything to get me back, especially now that my father ... my father ..." he choked back an embarrassing hoarseness "... may not be able to come back."

"I understand." Her own voice grew dark. "But I don't see how you can help them. They've got a very large ranch. Probably food and weapons. Certainly shelter. All we've got out here is ... each other."

Mundo rubbed his head. It still hurt some from the mighty blow Riley had given him with his carbine.

"Look," he said awkwardly, "there's a lot about my family you don't know. And even if you did, you probably couldn't understand."

The girl stepped back from him. Anger lit her deep brown eyes.

"We were having a wedding when we got word that the Texans had beaten our troops near Fort Craig. Everybody we know was at the ranch. Some of our relatives had come all the way from Mexico. Most of the men rode straight from the Roadrunner to join the Yankee troops. They left their families in our care." Furiously he battled a swell of tears. He would *not* let a Navajo see him cry.

"There aren't enough men left to fight anybody off. Do you understand? Not enough to save the guests. Not enough to save my sister. Not enough … to stop the Texans from what they did last time."

The girl looked down to give him privacy. He said nothing, but he was grateful.

Behind him, a flycatcher sang out its morning call. He could hear the rustle of tiny creatures—lizards, kangaroo rats?—scampering about.

"I still don't see how you can save them."

"I can't save Riley, either."

"You could try."

Mundo met her eyes squarely this time. "If I've got to make a choice—if I'm going to try to save anybody— it's going to be my sister."

The girl looked away. This time *she* looked as though

she were fighting tears. Mundo knew he was right, but still he felt ashamed.

"I need to know," the girl said slowly, "whether or not you'll really send help. I need to know if somebody will come."

"Of course I'll send someone," Mundo answered gruffly. "It just might take some time."

"Riley doesn't have any time!" she retorted harshly. "And if he dies, I need to know if I should wait here—" a sob escaped her, "wait here all alone."

It was Mundo's turn to stare at the ground. He had a sudden vision of this girl burying Riley, or deciding he was too hard to bury, deciding to wait here forever, deciding she had to go on.

He felt dirty. Deep-down-inside guilty. Mundo was surprised that a Navajo could make him feel that way. He regretted having to leave her alone out here with Riley, but his family had to come first.

"I'm sorry, but I've got to get to the Roadrunner just as fast as I can," he said as kindly as he could. "If you won't stay here, I'll have to take Riley with me. And the trip will maybe kill him as well as slow me down."

"You didn't believe I'd stay with him before."

"I believed it ... at first."

"Only when it was convenient. And once you returned to Riley, you forgot *me* altogether! I could have been lying dead out there for all you cared!"

Mundo couldn't argue with her. She hadn't seen him at his best, that was for sure. And since she was a Navajo, he wasn't sure her opinion of him mattered. But still, it bothered him that she had challenged his honor. It bothered him that he might have compromised it himself.

As he slung himself into the saddle, Mundo realized that the girl was standing at his left side. She wasn't clinging to his shoe the way Chayito had when he'd ridden off to war, but she was wearing the same desperate look.

If somebody left my sister out here alone to die, I'd track him to the ends of the earth, Mundo suddenly realized. He hadn't really given much thought to the Navajo's situation. He'd just been making promises to make it easier to leave.

No matter what Mundo did, Riley didn't have much of a chance.

But the girl did.

Slowly, carefully—because he'd never touched a Navajo before—Mundo leaned over and laid his hand on her shoulder. "If you promise to stay with Riley till he gets well or dies," he vowed, "I promise to send somebody back for you."

When Riley finally opened his eyes, the sun was beating down on him. His mouth felt like sand. Above all, he craved water. He looked for the canteen and remembered it was empty.

But he was relieved to find his carbine and cartridge box nearby. Last night he and Mundo had argued over who should keep the weapon, and he still wasn't sure why Mundo had given in. Riley was certainly in no condition to fight him.

He spotted the girl a few feet away on a chair-sized, tortoise-shaped rock not too far from where the bats hung upside down, jostling for position. She didn't move when he tried to sit up, but her brown eyes looked sympathetic.

"Mundo's gone?" he asked, already knowing the answer.

"He wanted to get an early start. He promised he'd send someone."

Riley couldn't bear to look at her. "You don't believe him."

She shrugged. "He said it as though he meant it."

"You still don't believe him."

She glanced at the corner of the ruins as two bats flew past Riley to join the others.

"I ... think we should plan to be here for a while. I thought I'd wait till you were up before I looked around."

Riley swallowed back his gratitude. She wanted to be sure he didn't think they'd *both* deserted him.

"He didn't have to come back for me yesterday," he said, lamely defending the Hispanic boy. "I meant, neither did you. But I'm thinking, if he did that, why would he forget me—us—today? And he left my gun. That must mean ..." As he realized what it probably meant, his voice trailed off.

The girl looked away.

"I believe," she said slowly, "that he will try. But I have been sitting here, thinking, since he left. And I have realized that whether or not he plans to come back is not the most important thing."

Riley tried to straighten up, folding his legs under him. It wasn't easy, and he knew he couldn't sit up too long. At least the crusty skirt-strips around his chest had finally dried.

"What is the most important thing?"

Uneasily she met his eyes. "When I was captured, I kept thinking, 'my father will come.'"

He nodded, not sure what to say. He'd never had a father. Well, he'd had Jake, who might have been his pa. In fact, he'd always figured that Jake must have had a powerful reason to take him in, since his widow had thrown Riley out just hours after her husband died. But it had always been a grudging kindness he'd received from Jake, not so much a display of affection as a sense of obligation. Would Jake have rescued him if he'd been stolen by Indians?

Maybe, Riley realized. But maybe not. Not if he'd had to explain it to his wife first.

"When I was a little girl, about three, the bluecoats came after us. All the women tried to herd us children away to safety, but when my mother hurried back for my little brother, I panicked. I ran the wrong way. I tried to figure out where my mother was, but I couldn't seem to find her. The bluecoats were close, so I ran into the hills and hid beneath a huge, rotted log."

Her voice was soft, almost blurry.

"I hid there, afraid to make a sound, the whole day. And the next. I snuck out that night to find some food, and some water. In an hour I was totally lost. It was a nightmare. I was alone for three or four days."

Riley was no longer sure of the point of this story. But there was some reason she was telling him, of that he was sure. Until now, he hadn't heard her say more than a dozen words back to back.

"What happened?" Riley asked.

A quick, bittersweet smile played across her lips.

"My father came. He was injured. He had been in battle. He had tracked down my mother and our relatives and taken them to safety. And then he had searched and searched for his little girl." Tears filled her eyes. "I waited. And he came."

Riley didn't understand. Maybe it was because he'd never had a father. Never had anybody cared enough about him to rescue him from any situation.

Except for Joey. If Joey'd been alive, Joey would have been out looking for him right now. Even if the sergeant had forbidden it, Joey would have come.

"You think he will come after you now?"

The girl shook her head. "My father is dead. He has to be. When I was taken captive, I waited and waited. I was sold. I *waited*. I was sold again. I waited. I turned nine and then ten and I waited." Her eyes looked black with sorrow. "I know he's dead. They're *all* dead, because *nobody ever came.*"

Riley couldn't think of a thing to say. He had to lie down. He was getting dizzy. He didn't understand this girl at all.

"I wasted all that time, waiting. Waiting when I could have been getting away, or planning my escape. Oh, I tried a few times, but . . . I gave up. I gave up too soon. *I was sure my father would come.* I knew he loved me. I knew he would never forget me as long as he was alive. It just did not occur to me, when I was so young, that something might keep him from coming." She stood up and faced the sun. Her voice grew dark. Her words were slow. "I realize now that he's been dead for a very long time."

"I'm sorry," Riley said, trying to face her as he stretched out on his side. "It must have been—"

"I did not tell you this story so you would feel sorry for me," she countered bluntly. "I told you so you would understand. *We cannot wait for Mundo.* He may keep his promise, if he is able. But there are rustlers out there, the *desert* is out there, and I don't really think he knows where he is going."

Shock stabbed Riley. "You don't think he'll forget us. You think he won't be able to come back."

Slowly, she nodded. "There are too many risks in the wilderness, for him and for us. We cannot leave here until you are fit to travel, so we must work very hard at finding some kind of food and water."

Before Riley could answer, she bent down to pick up his heavy carbine. Her hands trembled with the weight of it.

"I will learn to hunt," she said bravely. "You will teach me how to use your gun."

Chapter Sixteen

It was early afternoon by the time Mundo first saw the mountain. It sprang up all by itself in the desert, spiraling skyward like a grand church steeple. Its edges flattened down to the desert in little lumps of pine and cedar. The nearest lump was a good twenty miles away.

He was thrilled to see a landmark, any landmark, that would help him determine his location. It was hard to be certain he was going in the right direction with absolutely nothing to distinguish one mile of the flat land from another. He knew the Roadrunner Ranch—the whole valley, in fact—so well he could have drawn a picture of it in his sleep. So why hadn't he recognized a single clump of shale or odd-shaped cactus?

The truth was, he did not, just yet, recognize the mountain. But there were a few "lost mountains"—mountains that had been abandoned by some range and left to fend for themselves—in the dry basin between Albuquerque and Santa Fe. He had seen two or three of them. Surely when he got closer ...

But the mountain seemed taller and taller as he rode toward it, and within an hour Mundo knew he had never seen it before. It was no longer a matter of proving himself to the girl and Riley. They were all in terrible trouble if he was truly lost.

Carefully he pondered his situation. He'd tried to go straight north since the morning after the dust storm. If he'd traveled west by mistake, he would have circled back to the range near Albuquerque by now. That meant he'd somehow ended up far to the east. *Impossible,* he silently protested. *I always kept a sharp eye on the land!*

And then he realized what had happened. The night they had slipped away from the outlaws, they had all come roaring out of the canyon with no thought but escape. They could have gone in any direction, especially while they were fighting that terrible dust storm.

He decided to rest the horse. They were both too worn out and dry-mouthed to press on. And there wasn't any point in hurrying to a place that was all wrong.

But the buckskin did not want to stop. It was picking up energy, picking up speed. And as Mundo watched the twitch of its ears, he realized that the horse was neither heading toward the mountain nor toward what he now figured was home. It was heading in the wrong direction, toward the Staked Plains. East.

As tired and thirsty as the poor beast was, that could only mean one thing. It smelled water.

The buckskin started to jog, then to lope. After twenty minutes, it began to gallop. Mundo gave the horse its head and just held on.

By now he could see cottonwoods, all lined up in a

curving row. Here and there grew a desert-willow. Pockets of mesquite sprouted from the rich blue grama grass.

The final half mile, the buckskin ran with a wild, frenzied gait that mirrored Mundo's own desperation. Never had he been more thirsty! By the time he could see the water glistening through the willows, he was practically standing in his stirrups. The horse charged down into the stream and thrust its muzzle through a thin sheet of ice while the water swirled around its knees.

Mundo was horseman enough to drag the beast out of the water so he could dismount dryly, but he was too eager to wait that long himself. He practically jumped out of the saddle into the creek. Imitating the buckskin, he cracked the ice and began to drink.

He had never, ever, tasted water so cold or so incredibly good. He drank and drank and drank, drank until his stomach pooched out. When he finally pulled up out of the water, Mundo's nose felt numb with cold.

He smiled. He was shivering. He laughed out loud. There was nothing like water to make a man happy in the desert! It was almost as good as the sight of home.

When he saw Chayito and Julio and *El Patrón* in his mind, Mundo's smile grew thin. He hadn't accomplished anything. They still had not been warned. He still didn't know just where the ranch was—only where it wasn't. And Riley and the Navajo were no better off than they had been before.

He stood up, holding onto the reins just to be safe, and pondered his situation. It was obvious he was east of the Roadrunner, far east. He needed to go west, but he couldn't ride through the solitary mountain. That meant he either had to ride northwest, around the mountain, or southwest—basically back the way he'd come.

I can take the girl and Riley water, he realized. *Then they can move to this creek to wait.*

The intensity of his relief surprised him. Only now that he'd found a solution to his new friends' problem could he admit to himself how troubled he'd been by having to abandon them. They were helpless in the desert. They had nobody to count on but him.

He decided to move upstream to fill his canteen before he rode back to the ruins. Between Mundo and the horse, the water here was pretty churned up. And maybe he could find some kind of container to carry more of it with him. One canteen was hardly enough.

"Come on," he said to the horse, who was going to get sick if it drank any longer. Its belly already sagged. "Let's see what we can find."

There was, Mundo figured, no other water for miles in any direction. That meant people who knew the area would come here for water, camp here, maybe even build here eventually. There was a slight rise in the distance. Maybe he would spot a sheepherder from there . . . or even a cowboy!

Swiftly he heeled the horse into a jog beside the stream. Bloated now, and happy, it wasn't in the mood to hurry. But Mundo insisted, and it reluctantly complied.

They reached the rise in a few minutes. Mundo nudged the buckskin as far as it could go, then dismounted. He tied the creature to a sturdy willow, slung the empty canteen around his neck, and clambered up the slick bank.

At first, he could see nothing. No houses, no cattle, no camps. He cast a careful rancher's eye over the peaceful scene, trying to figure out what struck him wrong.

Then he saw it. Clear as day. *The water was muddy.* Upstream from where he and the buckskin had plunged in. It was churning with muck. Not the kind of dirt that a dust storm might add to a creek, but the kind that only comes from a herd of cattle—or horses.

They're here. He knew it at once. The outlaws had headed east with their booty, moving slowly but surely toward the only water in the area. They were headed toward the dry-as-death Staked Plains. They would stop at a stream first.

Mundo held his breath and listened. Yes, he could hear the herd. Long-legged bodies moving in the grass, the occasional neigh. Somewhere up ahead, there were horses. Did they belong to the Riveras and *El Patrón?*

He remounted the buckskin and moved along until he was so close he risked being seen. Then he slid off and tied the creature up again—to a cottonwood this time— and snuck up on foot. He was looking for outlaws, looking for evidence, and looking for any way at all that he could transport water.

Steadily he crawled forward. The sounds grew louder. The creek was congealed with mud.

Then he saw the first man. He was a stranger. He looked seedy, but in Mundo's eyes, so did every Texan.

He lowered himself to the ground and watched. In a few minutes another man—one he recognized from the canyon—sauntered up to the first one's side.

They started to talk. Mundo could see their lips

move, but he couldn't make out more than every other syllable. In frustration he snuck forward, one careful foot at a time.

But it was his feet he was watching, not the canteen which hung loose, swinging. Mundo didn't notice it until it slammed into a rock with a sharp ping.

Instantly the cowboys dived for cover. One of them drew his pistol and shot at Mundo.

They think it was a gunshot! he realized, heart thudding. *They know I'm here and they think I'm shooting at them!*

What would they do if they realized he wasn't even armed?

He couldn't risk hiding. They were too close, and the cover was too thin. He had one choice, and that was to reach his horse before the outlaws caught him. He stood, half-crouched, and began to run.

"There he is!" somebody shouted.

Blaaaam! fired another gun.

"Look, it's the kid! The one worth all the money!"

"Go tell Kurtzer!"

"Toland, this is your mess! I don't care what Kurtzer says! You clean it up or you're on your own!"

Mundo just kept on running. He ran and slid and dived down the rocks until he spied the buckskin, happily munching on some dandelions. The hungry beast didn't even raise its head.

He had just ripped loose the reins from the cottonwood when another gunshot rang out, this time from right behind him. Mundo bolted up on the horse as the bullet sailed past his head.

Chapter Seventeen

Tenchi spent most of the day searching for food, any kind of food, especially barrel cactus. She wasn't sure what other plants were good or safe, and she didn't find much that looked appealing. She was afraid to go too far from the ruins unarmed, keenly aware that she had no protection from the wild animals. If she got hurt, she'd never get back to Riley.

It had taken all of five minutes for both of them to realize that she couldn't use his gun. Riley wasn't strong enough to stand up and show her how to use it right, but that didn't matter because she wasn't strong enough to hold it steady. She was too short to easily reach the trigger.

Riley had draped his carbine over the tortoise-shaped rock and tried to show her how to aim it that way. He was incredibly good, even injured. He showed her how to fire five times, and every time he hit his mark.

He was very patient, but Tenchi soon realized she

was only wasting ammunition that Riley might use if he got better. Besides, the chance of a jackrabbit hopping by this particular corner of the ruins was pretty thin.

After last night's rest, Riley seemed a little stronger. There was no water to wash his wound, so Tenchi did not try to remove the blood-soaked yellow strips of skirt. She didn't know if the wound was infected, but at least it had stopped bleeding. And Riley didn't look quite so pale. Maybe, with food and water and determination, he would surprise them. But it was certainly too early to tell.

It was also, she decided a moment later when she saw a horse sauntering in their direction, too early for help to arrive. And, if Mundo had kept on heading north, it was coming from the wrong direction.

Tenchi crouched behind a stand of staghorn cholla, not yet certain if she should risk revealing herself. She and Riley would be better off asking almost anybody for help than they'd be waiting here alone. Any *stranger*. But they had not traveled very far from where they'd left the outlaws. And the outlaws were well mounted.

Silently she watched, all the while keeping an eye on Riley. He was lying down near the bats, asleep or nearly so, oblivious to the horse galloping toward him.

Riley shifted his legs and rolled over. By now she knew how often he looked dead or too limp to move when he was only trying to build his energy. What would he do, Tenchi wondered, if she told him there was trouble? Was he strong enough to do anything but fret?

She glanced back toward the man on the horse and realized that he had disappeared into a depression of land, probably an old, dry lake bed. Then she spied another mounted rider heading up out of the low place, closer to her, and this one she knew.

It was Mundo. Not Mundo riding out, strong and brave and proud, but Mundo slinking along like a weasel.

He's being followed, Tenchi realized. *Does he know it, or is he just worried?* She didn't know which was smarter—to call out to him that there was danger or hope the tracker would pass her by. There was no point in risking her hiding place, or Riley's. She was so far away that she wasn't sure Mundo could hear her if she shouted a warning.

Then she saw Mundo take one last look at the open ground and scattered buttes behind him, tie up his horse on a solitary ocotillo, and dart through the grass toward the ruins. A second later the man rode up out of the depression. He was close enough to recognize this time. Small mouth, missing tooth, cold expression.

It was Toland.

She was certain he saw Mundo, too.

"Mundoooo!" Tenchi screamed, suddenly aware that she could not hide like a mole while Toland killed him. *"Look out!"*

If he heard her warning, he gave no sign.

Mundo scrambled over the last few yards and slid into the ruins. He was certain he'd shaken Toland some time ago, but he couldn't be too sure.

He was sweaty and exhausted after his hard, scary ride, and he knew he was getting careless. Once before he had thought he'd lost Toland, only to have the outlaw show up and start firing at him. Clearly it was too late to bribe him with the offer of a Rivera's ransom. Toland had shot to kill.

Mundo carefully crawled around the walls toward the spot where he'd left Riley. He didn't want to admit that he'd come back with an empty canteen, but at least he'd brought news of water. *If only Riley could walk,* Mundo thought, *I could just point him and the girl in the right direction.* But when he reached the bats' open air bedroom, the Navajo wasn't there.

Riley was. He was half-lying on a tortoise-shaped rock near the pile of dried bat guano. His face was sweating. His hands shook. His carbine muzzle gleamed in the sun. It was pointed right at Mundo.

He's gone crazy, Mundo thought. *He's going to die and he wants to shoot me first. I should have known better than to try to befriend a Texan ... or a Navajo.*

He was certain it would be his last thought.

"Riley, I found a stream. I—"

"Freeze!" Riley hollered.

Instinctively, Mundo did.

Just then the gun went off.

It blasted so close to Mundo's face that he was sure it had hit him, and he couldn't understand why he didn't hurt anywhere on his body as he crumpled to the ground.

A second later another gunshot pinged by him, this one clattering off the top of the ruins' bat-filled corner.

He glanced once more at Riley, who no longer looked like an injured kid.

He looked like a Texas soldier.

Mundo turned to see where the other gunshot had come from. On the outskirts of the ruins, in a beeline behind him, lay the body of a man. Suddenly Mundo realized what had happened.

He'd never shaken Toland. He'd led him right back to his friends. But Riley—half-dead, good-for-nothing, proud-of-Texas Riley—had outwitted his own countryman.

And saved Mundo again.

Chapter Eighteen

Mundo tried to speak, but nothing came out of his mouth.

"Check him, Mundo," Riley ordered in a deadly soldier's tone. "Be sure he's dead. Take the gun."

Riley had to tell him twice before Mundo picked up the carbine, clumsily lifted it to his shoulder, and edged toward Toland. Toland's revolver lay at least a yard from his open hand. His lips twisted oddly, as though he'd died in pain. There was a gaping hole in his chest, but Mundo was taking no chances. For several silent moments, he just stood there, pointing Riley's carbine.

"I tried to warn you, Mundo," called Tenchi, who rather breathlessly ran up beside him. "I screamed as loud as I could. I thought ... I thought—"

She stopped as he stared at her. Mundo was relieved to see she was all right, but he didn't understand why the world's quietest girl was suddenly babbling. *She* wasn't the one who'd gotten stuck between Toland's gun and Riley's.

"Got your knife there?" he asked.

Still trembling, Tenchi nodded.

"Then keep it at the ready while I poke him with the gun." He raised his voice. "Do you hear that, Toland? If you try to jump me, she'll slit your throat." Mundo was about to add that she was, after all, a Navajo, and nobody could slit throats better. But something about the fear in Tenchi's face stopped him.

He understood. He was pretty shaken up himself. Only Riley seemed unfazed by the killing.

Mundo stuck his foot out and kicked Toland in the ribs. Nothing happened, so he kicked him again. He'd never killed a man, but he'd seen some Roadrunner cowboys die badly—a few at the hands of Navajos, several shot by Texans, and one crushed under a broken-legged horse. He was certain that Toland was no longer a threat. He couldn't say the same for the rest of the rustlers.

Mundo lowered the carbine and tried to hand it to Tenchi. "Why don't you cover me," he suggested more gently.

"I would, but I can't shoot that gun. Riley tried to teach me how this morning." She gazed suspiciously at Toland's revolver, then picked it up. "Maybe I can handle this, if I use both hands."

"Let me check it," Riley mumbled. He was still slumped over the rock.

"I can see if it's loaded," Mundo told him.

"Let me check it," Riley said again.

Mundo shrugged as Tenchi brought Riley the gun. It didn't seem worth arguing about. He'd never own a revolver and probably didn't know as much about firearms as a soldier. Still, he knew enough.

Riley checked it out, then handed it to Tenchi. "This is your weapon." He showed her how to hold and fire it. "It's not too heavy. You can carry it along. Mundo will get you the holster and you can wear it while you gather stuff." He gave her a faint smile. "You'll be safer now."

Mundo was surprised by the curious sort of family feeling that snuck into his heart. He felt protective, part-nered, proud. They had started off as three captured kids who didn't stand a chance. Somehow they'd stood together, bailed each other out, and outwitted the out-laws. In the process, they had become true friends.

Carefully handing the carbine back to Riley, Mundo straightened Toland's legs and reluctantly began to drag him away. He couldn't bear to look at the body.

Fighting nervous chills, he hid Toland in the rocks up the slope of the nearest butte. Anybody who really searched could find it, but unless somebody had tracked him this far, nobody would know where to look.

Tenchi trailed along behind him, but not closely. She said nothing, just shivered once or twice when Mundo pulled off Toland's gunbelt and handed it to her. She continued to follow him as he tracked down Toland's horse, which was grazing on some squirrel tail grass. Mundo was sure she shared his eagerness to put some distance between them and the body.

He found two canteens on the saddle, both almost full. Tenchi found army rations in the saddlebag. They shared a deep breath.

"Looks like we get supper tonight," Mundo said, grinning.

Tenchi smiled back. After a moment she replied,

"I'm sorry I wasn't more help with Toland. Navajos don't go near dead bodies ... or ghosts."

"It's all right. There wasn't much he could do to us anyway."

He asked Tenchi to ride the horse back, knowing she could use the practice. As he booted her up into the saddle, he couldn't help but notice *El Patrón's* brand on the animal's left shoulder. He wondered how much of the rustlers' herd was Roadrunner stock.

Mundo strapped the gunbelt around Tenchi's waist and helped her tuck the revolver into the holster. "Make sure you don't shoot yourself with that thing," he cautioned.

She grinned. An actual, honest-to-goodness happy grin! Mundo thought it changed her face completely. Every now and then, he even forgot she was a Navajo. It felt strange to think of a Navajo as a friend.

On foot, Mundo accompanied her back to the dead campfire. They found Riley stretched out again, half-covered with the blanket. His lanky face gave no hint that he'd just flat-out killed someone.

"How are you?" Tenchi asked as she swung off the horse.

"I'm a Texas soldier," he said wryly. "Reckon I'll do all right."

Tenchi smiled again, relief filling up her somber brown eyes. "I thought Toland was going to kill Mundo. I never dreamed you were well enough to help. This morning, Riley, you could barely hold that gun."

Riley shrugged. "Well, I can't take all the credit. I only figured out trouble was comin' 'cause you started shoutin', Tenchi. And I did have to brace the carbine on the rock."

"Still," pressed Tenchi, "I've watched cowboys and miners and soldiers shooting all my life, and you're a dead-eye shot."

"So it's been said," Riley bragged. "I was only so-so before I enlisted. For months after that all we had to do in camp was drill and practice shootin'. We was *determined* to get good at somethin', me and Joey."

Mundo didn't like the flow of the conversation. War and Texas. He tethered *El Patrón*'s stolen horse and asked Tenchi to go get Riley's buckskin, still tied to the ocotillo.

The minute the girl was gone, Mundo squatted down next to Riley. This was going to be hard to say, and he didn't want an audience.

"You always shoot like that?" he asked softly.

Riley shook his head. "I usually shoot standing up."

"So, you're … good. It wasn't just a lucky shot."

Riley's blue eyes narrowed. "The only thing lucky about it was that you had enough sense to hold still when you bumbled into the line of fire. When I first drew on Toland, you were nowhere to be seen."

Mundo looked away. "I tried to shake him. I thought I had. I didn't head back here until I was sure he couldn't follow me here."

"I noticed that," said Riley. His voice held no humor.

"Believe what you want. I'm telling you the truth. I found a stream. I was going to come back to bring you to it. Then I ran into the outlaws and had to make a run for it."

At first Riley didn't answer. Then into the silence, he accused, "You thought I was gonna shoot you." He was trembling with anger.

"I was just surprised."

"No, you wasn't. You thought I'd flat-out shoot you after all you done for me! You think I'm that kind of scum."

"What do you expect?" Mundo burst out. Their truce was wearing a little thin. "You're a Texan!"

"And what exactly does that mean?" Riley pressed. "This goes deeper than the war. You hated me clear down to your bones before we even spoke. You kept hollerin' that I'd killed your mama, your kin, folks I ain't never met." He jerked himself into a sitting position, looking pale but furious. "None of our troops ain't even reached your precious Roadrunner Ranch!"

"Not this time! And this time *you won't*." Mundo couldn't hide the scars on his heart. It made no sense to him, feeling gratitude to a boy for saving his life who had planned—and was still planning—to make war on his people.

Riley kept right on staring at him.

At last Mundo said, "I owe you, Riley. I'm grateful you saved my life. You and I . . . well, it's different between us. We're friends." Slowly he shook his head. "But I'll never change my mind about the rest of the Texans."

Chapter Nineteen

Riley didn't say much when Tenchi came back. She was leading the horse and carrying some spindly ocotillo stems in her skirt. Between the shredded blue cotton and the holster on her hip, Riley had never seen a girl look so funny, but he didn't dare laugh.

Mundo helped her stack the puny wood against the half-crumbled stone wall, then started a fire.

Later, they all ate with quiet pleasure. It was foreign fare to Tenchi and Mundo, but Riley knew Confederate Army rations all too well ... bone-hard crackers and salt-jerked meat. He never thought he'd rejoice in the taste-less stuff. *It's amazing,* he thought, *how great something bad can be just because it comes from home.*

The food, along with the rest of the day's events, eased the tension. When they had finished eating—and draining one of Toland's two canteens—they remained close to the fire. The wind was up and sneaking through the walls again. The bats were heading out.

"If Toland followed you, Mundo," commented Riley, "so can somebody else, come daylight. I don't think it's safe to stay here after tonight."

"But you can't ride yet, Riley," Tenchi protested. "Look how much you've improved with just one day's rest!"

"It's not worth the risk. We were lucky today. Really lucky. Without that rock, I would have been too wobbly to make that shot in my condition. Even so, I couldn't have set up for it in time if he'd seen me."

"I thought you were the best shot in the whole Texas army," Mundo reminded him.

"Sergeant said I was a natural," he had to admit, "but right now I'm sure not at my best."

Tenchi said to Mundo, "I don't think you're at your best, either. From all that bragging you did in the beginning, I didn't expect you to let Toland tail you." She was almost smiling. "On top of that, you got lost."

"I did not get lost!"

Riley howled and Tenchi chuckled. At first Mundo was indignant, but finally even he broke into a grin.

Riley felt good for the first time since he'd been shot. How great it was to laugh out loud with a couple of friends!

Mundo wanted to describe every detail of his adventure. Tenchi recalled one of her own, and Riley dug up a few tall tales. One thing led to another, and they kept on telling jokes and stories. They bragged about things that didn't matter and swapped age-old complaints about insect bites and the weather. It reminded Riley of the many nights he'd spent by a campfire with his soldier buddies. In spite of everything, he was having fun.

Even when the coals glowed white and red, Riley didn't want to break the spell. But he'd been taught that whenever an officer went down, somebody—the next in rank—had to fill his boots. The three of them had started out without a leader. They hadn't even been a group. But now they were, and somebody had to take charge of things. Mundo was used to giving orders. Tenchi was used to following them. But Riley was the oldest and had the most experience outrunning men chasing him with guns. He felt the need to "take command of his unit," at least until they all were safe.

"We gotta come up with a new plan."

Mundo answered, "There's nothing wrong with the old one. It just ... will take a little more time."

Riley shook his head. "If I can shoot a man, I can ride. I think we should all leave together."

Tenchi's eyes met Riley's, then Mundo's. "All of us?" The relief in her voice was hard to bear.

Riley nodded. "We've got two horses now, both freshly watered. One of you can ride with me if I'm really rocky. But truly—" he exaggerated, "I'm a lot better now."

"A *lot*?" repeated Mundo.

He smiled thinly. "All right. A little. Enough that I don't think I'll really slow you down."

"That's a lot of improvement in one day," observed Mundo. "I don't think you're ready for the hard trip I have in mind."

Riley didn't point out that he didn't think Mundo

was ready either. Tenchi was right about the tremendous risks any solitary traveler faced in the desert. And Mundo still wasn't entirely sure how far it was to the Roadrunner. He'd managed to let Toland follow him, and more than once he'd ridden off in the wrong direction.

Mundo was going to need help getting home.

"We're all leaving in the morning," Riley declared abruptly.

Riley expected Mundo to argue with him. But it was Tenchi who spoke up.

"Kurtzer will come after Toland."

The two boys stared at her.

"What?" they said together.

"When Toland doesn't come back, Kurtzer will follow him. When he finds out you killed him, Riley, he will kill you. Or die trying."

A ghost of wind swept over the fire.

"That's a pretty wild guess, Tenchi," countered Mundo. "I don't—"

"I was with them a whole day before you got there. They thought I could cook, just because I was a girl. I *listened.*"

Riley felt light-headed again. He had to lie down.

"Go on," said Mundo.

"Most of the men were in Kurtzer's unit. They came up the Rio Grande from Texas together. They thought their officers were snooty and stole all the food. They got bored waiting for the war to start. They were always too hot or too cold. Finally they deserted."

Riley's eyes look troubled. "Every soldier's got his problems. Ain't no reason to turn your back on your flag."

Mundo lay one hand on Riley's arm, as though to stop him.

"It was Kurtzer's idea," she continued. "He was sort of a bully, always causing trouble. He'd been punished several times and decided he'd had enough."

"*Go on,*" repeated Mundo.

"It was all planned. They were going to sneak off on their way past Fort Craig, you know, the day of the big battle."

"I was there," said Riley.

He felt Mundo stiffen beside him. Mundo took his hand off Riley's arm.

"Anyway, some Yankees started firing unexpectedly. They shot back and ran. They got mixed up with another unit on the way."

"It happens." Riley's voice was dry.

Mundo stood up and took a few steps away.

"Toland was in the other unit. He saw a Yankee—a New Mexican—aiming to fire at Kurtzer. Kurtzer had just used up his ammunition and was trying to reload. He couldn't draw."

"Toland shot the enemy," said Riley.

"The *New Mexican.*" Mundo's voice was grim.

"Toland saved his life. He talked Toland into coming with them. The other outlaws resented the fact that Kurtzer was still trying to pay back Toland. He gave him chances, let him have his own way, everything."

Tenchi took a deep breath and kept going. "Toland wasn't big on killing like some of the others were. He was perfectly willing to rob New Mexicans, but he shied away from shooting fellow Texans."

"No wonder Toland didn't shoot Riley right off," said Mundo sharply. "Maybe he's not such a great shot after all."

"It was a perfect shot, and it saved your bacon, Rich Boy," snapped Riley.

"I saw everything, Mundo," Tenchi declared. "Toland didn't see him. He didn't see me. His gun went off a second after Riley's." Slowly she added the obvious. "If Riley hadn't outgunned him, you'd be dead."

"Thought I was, for a minute there," murmured Mundo. The resentment in his voice still lingered. "Looked like Riley was aiming right at me."

Chapter Twenty

After that, the mood changed, and Tenchi didn't want to stay at the fire any longer. She went for a walk, circling the ruins and checking on the horses, keeping her revolver safely in its holster. She made sure not to go near the body of Toland. She had not forgotten *everything* she had learned as a child. Terrible things happened when ghosts crossed paths with Navajos.

"What do you think?"

She jerked around at the sound of the voice. Relief wrapped around Tenchi like a warm blanket when she realized it was Mundo.

"You've been with Riley all day. Is he all mouth, or do you think he's well enough to travel?"

From the top of the butte, a screech owl announced itself to anyone who would listen. Another night bird, with a sweeter tone, quickly replied.

"I thought he would be dead by now," Tenchi slowly

answered. "But he's starting to get better. We really only stayed before because you wouldn't take us with you."

It was blunt, but truthful.

"Why can't we all go? We've got two horses now."

There was another long silence. Then Mundo said, "I meant it, Tenchi, when I promised to come back."

It was the first time he had ever called her by her name. It made her pleased and angry. It made her suspicious, too.

"You were chased back."

"*I meant it.*" Another awkward silence trapped them. Then Mundo said, "If Riley's so hot to travel, maybe he should go find his precious Texas army. You come with me."

Her eyes widened, but he pressed on. "I just remembered, listening to him brag, how hard it's going to be explaining Riley to my family. It's not just the war, Tenchi. I've been taught to hate Texans all my life. You don't know what they've done to my family. *Mi mamá*—" he stopped, choking on the word. "They killed my mother when I was a baby," he confessed awkwardly. "And they didn't stop with her."

Tenchi understood what it was like to lose a mother. But she also knew what group of people had taken Tenchi's mother from *her*. Her hatred for Mundo's people ran as deeply as his hatred for Riley's.

"The men who kidnapped me were New Mexicans," she told him. "Since then I have lived as a captive, a slave, for people of the same race, or for the Yankees. I learned long ago I could not spend my life hating everyone. I kept my hatred for the ones who stole me. And killed my loved ones."

"Nobody at the Roadrunner ever launched a raid against the Navajos," Mundo retorted. "Though more than once we had to chase some of them to retrieve our horses."

"That is different," she said simply. "It is war. It is life. It is the way my people survive."

"Not anymore. We've just about finished off the Navajos, at least the wild ones. And the ones like you that are servants are treated not too badly, all things considered."

"'Not too badly!' says the rich boy! Have you ever thought for one minute what it would be like to be a slave?"

"I'm a Rivera," he answered sharply. "I will never have a reason to consider life as a slave."

"Well, I was not born to be so lucky. I've been sold and passed from one owner to another. Some of them were kind. Others treated me like a chicken whose job was to lay them eggs. The day the outlaws found me I was on the way to be a gift to some prissy bride about to marry the son of *El Patrón*."

Mundo's eyes opened wide.

"I once talked to a Navajo who had been *El Patrón*'s slave. He is kind to no one! He treats his own wife as a servant! And she comes from a wealthy Hispanic family. Can you imagine what life would be like for me if I had not been captured by the rustlers and managed to escape?"

Mundo was staring at her with a deep shock on his face that made no sense to Tenchi. He had lived here all his life. He knew how his people treated Navajos. He claimed his father was as rich as *El Patrón*. The Riveras probably had Indian slaves of their own. Why should her words so greatly surprise him?

Night crawled over the ruins in earnest. Tenchi could hear tiny creatures crawling out. A distant coyote howled.

But she could see nothing. Of course, a ghost was not a being one would see.

The silence grew worse. Harsh in its emptiness. Tenchi knew that something was enormously wrong with Mundo, but she did not know what to do about it.

Finally she asked in a small voice, "What is it?"

"The rustlers," he answered tightly. "Did they kill anyone when they . . . found you?"

She nodded. "Two Yankee cowboys."

"Just Yankees?"

"Yes. They were carrying me to the ranch in a wagon with some dry goods they picked up in Santa Fe. I was one of the 'presents'—" the words stuck in her mouth, "to be delivered for the great wedding."

Mundo reached out both arms to hold her shoulders. He looked into her eyes as though her next words would determine his life or death.

"Did they hurt anybody else after they killed the cowboys? Did they hit a herd or a flock or . . . the headquarters of a ranch?"

His hands were trembling. He was gripping her hard.

"No. They were supposed to be collecting the herd that *El Patrón* was sending to the bride's father. But all they could find was the wagon, and *El Patrón*'s men. I convinced them I was worth too much money to kill." She straightened a little. "I *am* a weaver, you know. A very fine one."

Mundo dropped his hands. His mouth fell open into a tiny "o." He stared at Tenchi, then rubbed his hand over his face.

"Mundo, what is it? Tell me!"

He shook his head.

"How can it get any worse?"

He sucked in air. He breathed it out again.

At last he spoke. "I didn't know, Tenchi. When I promised to take you back to the ranch, to get help. I was so afraid for my family, so afraid for myself. I didn't realize . . ."

"Tell me. *Tell me!*" she ordered.

"The night before we left for Albuquerque, the festivities for my sister's wedding were scheduled to begin. Everybody was riding in. One wagon broke down. It never showed up." At last his eyes met hers. "It belonged to *El Patrón*."

"*El Patrón!*" she whispered.

"We were worried about warriors as well as Texas outlaws," Mundo rushed on. "Along with the wedding gifts they were bringing—" he took a deep breath, "a Navajo weaver from Santa Fe, about my sister's age."

It took Tenchi a long, dark moment to understand. *She* was the slave meant for Mundo's sister? His family was about to connect with that of the great and powerful *El Patrón? Mundo planned to take her back to the Road-runner Ranch where she would live the rest of her life as his sister's slave?*

"No wonder you were always ordering me to stay with Riley!" she blurted out. "You never once thought of me as a friend. To you I am nothing but a slave!"

"That's not true!" Mundo insisted. "I didn't know you were my sister's gift until ... just now. I've had too much to think about. I'll admit that at first I had trouble thinking of you as ... well, a person. But we're friends now, Tenchi. Honestly."

Tenchi tried to believe him. She *wanted* to believe him. But the anger was slow to subside.

"If we are friends, how can you take me back to *El Patrón*? How can you expect me to go back to slavery ... to be the gift of his son's lazy new bride?"

"My sister is not lazy!" Mundo barked. "She's the hardest-working person I know. She was only a baby when our mother died, but she started running the house years ago! You are lucky—do you hear me, *lucky!*—to go live with her! She'll take care of you. She is clever enough to protect you from *El Patrón*. Your life will be a thousand times better than it would ever be anywhere else! You know you can't make it as a real Navajo!"

Wildly Tenchi pulled away from him. The words bit at her soul, all the more deeply because they were proba-bly true. Even if she could ever find her way back to her people, she no longer knew how to live with them. They would laugh at her! Worse yet, they would not accept her at all. *My parents are dead,* her heart reminded her. *All the Navajos I once loved are dead or were captured long ago.* There was no other reason why she had remained a captive.

Still, she could not bear to give up after only two days of freedom!

Tears crept, then poured, down her wide-cheeked face as she ran from Mundo. She ran out into the desert, away from the ruins of the village, away from the ruins of her dream. It was over. She would die out here, or she would become Mundo's sister's slave. He probably hadn't planned it that way, but she knew their friendship could never be the same if she was owned by his kin.

Far behind her, Tenchi could hear Mundo calling her name. A moment later she heard Riley yelling, too. And then, with no warning whatsoever, she heard the stone walls of the ruins shaking.

The earth rumbled as well. It sounded as though two giants had taken hold of it and were tugging in opposite directions, ripping it apart.

The land beneath her was no longer strong and sturdy. It was nothing but a great dry puddle of sand. She could not run, could not move, could not even stand still! The earth shook her until she lost all strength in her legs and arms, shook her until she fell.

As Tenchi went down, she heard Riley call out once more, this time shouting her name in warning. Then she heard the banging of the stacked rocks that had served the three of them as shelter. They crashed into each other, bouncing from one hard surface to another, as they tumbled off their unsteady perches down to sagebrush and sand.

Chapter Twenty-One

"Tenchi! Mundo! Is everybody all right?" hollered Riley when he was sure the stones had stopped falling.

At first there was no answer. He wasn't quite sure where his friends were. They'd both been heading for the horses before he'd last dozed off. But he'd heard Mundo yelling at Tenchi, pleading, maybe, in his almost-arrogant tone. She hadn't answered.

The walls had tumbled. A thousand more rocks lay on the ground. There was no trace of Mundo's fire, nothing left of the bats' daytime home. Suddenly Riley guessed why the Indians who had built this village had been forced to leave it.

"Mundo! Tenchi!" he called again.

This time, Riley got an answer.

"I'm over here!" It was Tenchi. "Are you all right?"

"Fine. Shaken up a bit—" he pushed aside a rock that had bloodied his face, then crawled to his feet, "but I've been through worse."

By now he could see her coming, almost running toward him. She was trembling, and Riley couldn't blame her. He'd grown up with hurricanes, tidal waves, and deadly floods near the Gulf of Mexico, but he'd never felt the earth shake like this.

"You aren't hurt?"

She shook her head. "I was out in the grass. No rocks near me. So was Mundo—"

"No, I heard him calling you. Then he called to me to see if you'd come back to the fire. He was looking for you on the other side of the ruins when I went to check the horses."

Tenchi's face wrinkled up. "It's my fault. I was yelling at him—"

"I heard. What was that all about?" Before she could speak, Riley said, "Never mind. Not now. We've got to find him first."

They headed back toward the rubble. It was hard to crawl over the rocks and even worse trying to move them. Riley was afraid they'd step on Mundo. They couldn't seem to find him.

"Mundo! Mundo! *Muuundooo!*" Tenchi cried out repeatedly.

There was no answer.

She turned to face Riley. "It's bad. Isn't it?"

He turned away. "Let's just find him first. He could be unconscious." He didn't add the obvious: *He could also be dead.*

They searched for twenty minutes before they found a hill-shaped rubble large enough to hide a boy. They had no proof that Mundo was lying beneath it.

There just didn't seem to be any other place big enough to conceal him.

Suddenly the earth began to shake again. This time it was Riley who screamed. Tenchi fell against him. They both landed on the rock pile that they feared hid their friend.

"We've got to find him!" Tenchi whispered as soon as the aftershock had passed. "It could get worse. If he's still alive—"

"Of course he's still alive," muttered Riley. "He's too stubborn not to be. We just have to find him." Ten minutes ago he'd felt too weak to sit up, let alone do arduous work, but now he knew he had to find the inner strength that had blindly carried him through battle.

Already he was thinking like a soldier. Protect the living; put their safety over that of the dead. If there was no hope for Mundo, Riley and Tenchi needed to take both horses and ride out of here like crazy. Someday he would get word to Mundo's family, maybe even come back here to bury him.

But if Mundo was still alive, somebody had to go get help and somebody had to stay with him. Tenchi knew little about the desert and could barely sit a horse, but Riley was the only one strong enough to wrestle these enormous rocks. He knew it would be incredibly difficult in his condition, but he never considered turning away from the job.

The moon was bright, but it was still hard to see much. One by one, with tremendous effort, Riley pulled the lighter rocks off and dragged them away from the pile. Tenchi tried to help, but she didn't have enough muscle to do much.

Suddenly she stopped. Riley watched her poke her hand down between two flat stones.

"What are you doing? Trying to lose your fingers?"

"I thought I saw something! Skin, maybe."

She stopped, leaned forward, pressed herself against the pile of rocks and dug down deeper.

"It's Mundo's nose!"

Riley's stomach heaved in relief. He gestured for her to move, then pulled off another rock. Belatedly he realized that, in his hurry, he had probably scraped Mundo's face. He could see an opening now, big enough that—if he were still alive—Mundo could probably breathe.

He tried to reach down, to feel Mundo's throat, but his hand was too big.

"Can you touch him? Feel his pulse?" he asked Tenchi.

She edged up beside him, lay gingerly on the rocks, and stuck her hand down through them once more. At first she said nothing. Then she whispered, "I'm getting a beat. At the base of his throat. At least I think so. It might be my own heart. It's pounding."

"You have to be sure!" Riley told her. He'd checked a hundred heartbeats since he'd joined the army, and he could tell in an instant whether a man was alive or dead. At the moment he wished Tenchi had had the same experience.

"Be quiet. Let me concentrate."

He waited. Off toward the butte where Toland's body lay came the eerie cry of an elf owl.

Riley was afraid.

But not for himself. Mundo still had a chance, and as long as he did, Riley would risk his own life to save him. He knew he'd rather die than bury another friend.

Night fell quickly in the desert. Toland's horse stopped to browse whenever it could, and Tenchi had a hard time keeping it moving. Mundo, she knew, would have had no difficulty getting it to do whatever he wanted.

Mundo was not afraid of the land, of the ghosts, of the distant howling of coyotes or wolves. Even when he did not know how to get home, he *thought* he did. He never lost his confidence. Maybe, Tenchi thought, it was because he'd always had a home to go to.

As fatigue crept into her legs and her eyelids became heavy, Tenchi realized that, at this moment, she had what she'd always thought she wanted: a real chance to escape from her captors and head toward Navajo land. Nobody knew where she was, nobody was looking for her, and anybody who had found *El Patrón*'s murdered cowboys probably thought she was dead.

But Tenchi quickly brushed away the temptation. She had forgotten many things about her childhood, but some things lay deep in her soul. One of them was that no Navajo ever abandoned an injured comrade. The tribe—the family—always came first.

How odd, she thought, that only yesterday she'd decided she was not brave enough to cross this desert alone! Tenchi could not risk the journey for herself, but she would risk it for a friend.

And not any friend, but the one whose sister would soon be Tenchi's master.

"We'll have to ride all night," she told the plodding horse. "Get a move on!"

She kicked the weary beast hard, hard enough to get it going. As the moon grew high, Toland's horse kept up a steady jog. It might have kept going all night if it had not, on the rough earth cloaked by darkness, plunged its right front hoof into a prairie dog hole.

When Mundo came to, he wished he hadn't. Someone was trying to drown him, and he felt as though he were stuck beneath an enormous pile of rocks.

He struggled to come out of the dream, but it just got worse. He gagged on the water. The pain in his legs was unbearable, even worse than the weight on his chest. He *had* to be dreaming. If he hurt this much in real life, he wouldn't be alive.

The water stopped pouring down his throat when he coughed mightily and heaved some of it up.

"Are you awake? Can you hear me?"

He knew the voice. A Texan drawl. Maybe he wasn't dreaming.

"Mundo, look at me. How many men do you see?"

Mundo blinked and turned ever so slightly. His

head throbbed. So did his neck. He saw one man. One Texan.

It was Riley.

"What happened?" he whispered as Riley put a stopper in the canteen and tossed it aside.

Riley was leaning over him at an odd angle, one foot anchored on solid ground several feet away. Mundo had never seen a person stretch into such an awkward position.

"There was an earthquake. We're camped out in the ruins, remember? Some more of the rocks came down."

"All of them on me?"

He closed his eyes before Riley could answer. The sun was high and it would have poured into Mundo's face if Riley's shaggy hair hadn't blocked it.

"Well, not all of them, but as much as makes no never mind." Riley pulled off his blood-stained Confederate jacket and rolled it up. Almost gently, he pushed it under Mundo's head.

Chapter Twenty-Two

The next time Mundo awoke, he found Riley trying to free his legs. He'd peeled off his blood-caked longjohn shirt. Mundo could see his thin, bandaged chest and his tightly muscled arms. He was sweating profusely.

The piles of rocks were higher on both sides, but so far Riley had only freed Mundo's upper half. He labored to move each stone. Mundo was accustomed to thinking of his friend as weak and helpless. Now he realized that Riley, despite the effect of his gunshot wound, was a very strong young man. And a tough one.

He was, Mundo remembered grimly, a Texas soldier.

"You get that strong slinging bullets at Yankees?" he asked.

Riley tried to laugh. "Hauling in two-hundred-pound marlins, more like it."

"A two-hundred-pound fish? Come on! I'm not stupid. That's a Texas tall tale if I ever heard one."

This time Riley really did laugh. "You ain't much of a fisherman. Don't find marlins close to shore very often. But me an' Jake once caught a big ol' fella that big."

"Not a chance."

Riley shoved another stone loose. He didn't seem inclined to talk. But Mundo couldn't bear to just lie there like a dead stump. The pain in his right knee was overwhelming. He needed some distraction.

"How long has it been since the earthquake?" Mundo asked. "Was I out very long?"

"All night and then some. With any luck Tenchi should reach your place today."

"Tenchi's on her way to the Roadrunner? Alone on a horse? I hope she at least took the revolver!"

"Yep. She headed out the minute we found you."

The terrible pain in Mundo's knee seemed to ease some. Help was coming! He tried not to think about how long it might take. Tenchi would bring Julio! A week ago, *Papá* would have come to save him. But *Papá* was ...

"You told her to ask for my brother?"

"She knows what to do."

"You sound pretty confident. Didn't you tell me just yesterday she was the 'worst dang-fool excuse for an Indian' you'd ever seen?"

Riley chuckled at Mundo's fake Texas accent. "I think *you're* the one who said that. Or something along those lines."

"She's got courage, Riley, and determination. But she can barely ride. She doesn't know the land." Abruptly Mundo remembered his last words to Tenchi before the earthquake. He'd been tactless, if not downright cruel. Now he was worried, for his new friend as much as himself. She had so few survival skills! "She'll be lucky to reach the Roadrunner alive."

Riley didn't answer. He pressed one shoulder against the huge doorway stone pinning Mundo's knee. Every muscle in his chest and arms quivered. With all his strength, it still didn't budge.

He leaned back on his heels and took a deep breath. "I just can't get that one, Mundo. I've tried and tried. At least you can breathe better. You want some more water?"

Mundo studied the rock. It was a good two feet by four feet, much heavier, he figured, than the fattest Gulf Coast marlin. The pressure it put on his knee was terrible. He was afraid the stone had crushed something.

"You gotta get it off. Julio might not get here until tomorrow or the next day."

"Mundo, I hate to say this, but I been workin' at this a long while." Riley's drawl grew soft. "I done used up more strength than I got. And one man would never be strong enough to push that dang-fool thing off anyway."

"Try."

"I have tried! I've tried for hours. I can't do it!"

"Try again!" Mundo was desperate.

"If I keep trying, I'm likely to dislodge all the rest of these stones. I don't want them coming down again all over you!"

"So you want me to just … lie here? Waiting for help to come? Wait here till my bones are crushed or I die?"

This time when Riley looked at him, there was no

humor in his blue eyes. Shame darkened Mundo's cheeks as he realized how many times in the past few days Riley had been left to die or wait for uncertain rescue. He knew what Mundo was feeling, how awful it was to be in terrible trouble and not be able to do a thing to help himself.

"You want some more water?" Riley offered. "I could use some." He took a quick drink, stopping himself, Mundo noticed, before he'd taken very much.

"My mouth sure is dry," Mundo admitted. "Try not to spill it all over me."

Riley grinned. "You used to havin' somebody wait on you?"

"Not all the time," Mundo answered. Then he smiled back. "Just most of it."

Riley laughed. Then he helped Mundo drink, cupping one hand under Mundo's neck. Mundo tried to hold on to the canteen himself but he couldn't seem to control his trembling fingers. Riley gently pushed Mundo's hands away but made sure Mundo got plenty.

"When do you think Julio will get here?" Mundo blurted out when he was finished.

"Hard to say."

"You do think Tenchi will be able to find her way there? And show Julio how to get back?"

Riley didn't reply. Mundo knew he was asking questions that had no answers.

He tried another tack. "If you're just going to sit there, can you talk to me? Keep my mind off things?"

"Don't have no more thrillin' stories to share. Gave up all my best tall tales last night."

"Tell me about your home. Before the army. When you were little."

Riley whistled. "Well, that won't take long. I was born. A fisherman took me in. His wife threw me out when he died. End of story."

Mundo wasn't sure if he was kidding. "This Jake fellow?" he prodded.

"Hmmm."

"Tell me about it."

"You don't care. I ain't gonna bleed my heart all over the place just to keep you entertained."

That's when Mundo realized Riley was serious. The story wasn't made up, and it wasn't that old. Whatever had happened with Jake and his wife had really hurt him.

"I'd like to hear it," he said truthfully.

Riley studied him for a minute. Then he said, "I ain't no rich kid like you. And I don't got nobody who's gonna come lookin' if I disappear. Not anymore."

"Who would have come?"

"Joey, my best friend. He was a fisherman's kid. We grew up on the docks together. He had real folks, but they didn't worry about him none. We took care of each other."

Mundo waited. There was nothing else for him to do.

"I don't know who my ma was. I'm not sure why Jake took me in. My best guess is that he knew her by going someplace his wife didn't approve of—a saloon maybe, or worse. When she got into trouble, he felt the need to help her out. I don't know whether she died or just left town. Jake only used the word 'gone' to describe her. His wife just called her 'sinful.'" He gave a bitter chuckle. "When I was knee-high to a grasshopper, I thought that 'Sinful Female' was her name."

Mundo couldn't laugh. He hurt all over, on the out-side, and now he hurt on the inside for Riley, too.

"About nine months ago, I lost Jake overboard. High wind, choppy waves. No worse than a dozen other days we'd fished those waters. Just bad luck.

"I searched all day for him. So did Joey and some of the other fishermen. There was no sign. Sometimes it's like that in the ocean. No trace of a man."

"Sometimes it's like that in the desert, too," Mundo offered.

Riley ignored him. "It was nigh unto midnight when I got home. She was standing there, Jake's wife, in the middle of the kitchen. She looked fierce-mad at me, madder than she'd ever been. I wasn't sure whether she'd heard about Jake or was just frettin' 'cause she'd had to keep supper on the table late."

"'He went overboard,'" I told her. "'We looked all day. There ain't no more to do.'"

"She didn't say a thing, just stared at me with those terrible eyes. At first I thought it was grief I was lookin' at. It wasn't till later I figured out it was pure hate.

"'I'm awful sorry, ma'am,' I said, remembering to call her what she liked. Then I started walkin' toward my room. Well, not *my* room exactly. I shared it with her boys. Two older, one younger. Her and Jake also had two girls."

Now Riley's voice dropped, as though he weren't really talking out loud. Mundo could barely hear, but he didn't want to say so.

"I was almost there, hand on the knob, when she said to me, 'Get out.' I couldn't believe I'd heard her right. She'd never, you know, babied me none, but she had raised me up.

"'Ma'am?' I said. 'You heard me. He's gone, and I don't have to burn with the shame he brought me for one day longer! *Get out of my house.*'"

Riley studied his hands. Mundo had never noticed before how knocked up and scarred they were. Fisherman's scars, he guessed, weren't all that different from those of a longtime cowboy.

"Two of the boys came out of our room. In the kitchen, I saw the oldest girl. I waited for one of them to say something, to calm their mother down. Nobody spoke. Finally the youngest boy walked over to Jake's wife and took hold of her skirt. From the kitchen the girl said softly, 'You heard our mama.'"

Mundo couldn't bear to look at Riley.

"I just took off. Spent the night in the boat. Next day, I talked Joey into goin' off to join the army. They was enlistin' men in a town nearby. He wanted excitement. I wanted to belong. We both wanted to fight for Texas. I ain't got no family, and I ain't got Joey no longer, but as long as I've got the army, I've got me a home."

Mundo was ashamed. He'd asked Riley to start this story just to keep him from dwelling on his own problems. Now he'd opened old sores of Riley's own.

"What happened to Joey?" he asked, hoping against hope that there was one person in Riley's whole life who hadn't let him down.

"Some Yankee shot him dead at Valverde, right

after we passed Fort Craig." Slowly he gazed at Mundo. "Well, I thought he was a Yankee at the time. You steered me different. He was actually a fellow who spoke Spanish and looked a lot like you."

Mundo had no reply. "I'm sorry," he said lamely. "I guess these things happen in war." It was a stupid answer, but he could think of nothing better.

The silence grew thick between them for five seconds, or maybe ten, until the earth once more began to rumble.

Chapter Twenty-Three

Riley should have run. Instead he threw his body forward, covering Mundo's face. Mundo grunted at the impact, then screamed when falling rocks bounced off the ones already pinning his legs. A few of them also hit Riley.

Riley took a deep breath. It could have been much worse. It was obvious that he couldn't leave Mundo here any longer. Anything could happen in the next aftershock.

Carefully he pulled himself off of Mundo. "Are you all right?"

Mundo started to chuckle, but his frightened laugh quickly turned into a sob. He was in such bad shape he didn't even look embarrassed.

"Listen to me, Mundo. We're going to move that stone. We're going to get you out of here," Riley promised, desperate to stop the tears.

"You said you couldn't do it alone."

"Well, I was wrong," Riley lied. "There has to be a

way to do it. I'm just not smart enough to think of it myself. Help me come up with something."

Mundo stopped crying, but a dead glaze slid over his eyes. Riley had seen that look on the faces of all too many wounded men. Once they gave up, there was no way to help them. They always died.

"Think out loud with me. What do we have to work with? You know this land. What's out there that's strong enough to use as some sort of lever?"

"Nothing. If there was, we would have used it by now for the fire. The only piece of timber within twenty miles that's strong enough to be a lever is your carbine, and—"

"Of course!" Riley fought back his sudden jubilance. "My gun! Nothing's stronger. I should have remembered. My sarge always said—" He broke off as he studied Mundo. "Lookee here. You've got to sit up. Get anchored with your hands in the dirt. Dig that one foot in the ground. Start getting ready. When I come back with the carbine, I'm going to use it as a lever while you pull yourself out."

"What if your gun breaks?" Mundo sounded terrified.

"It won't." Riley tried to smile. "It's never let me down."

On that note he bolted off to find his carbine, still lying on the edge of the rubble. How could he have forgotten it?

Riley knew that even if Mundo managed to pull himself out in time, the doorway stone would crush the gun. And if Mundo wasn't strong enough, or quick enough, or the rock was just too heavy . . . Riley would be out on the desert alone again.

He could wait for Tenchi, of course, but he wasn't counting the minutes till she arrived. He'd heard what she'd said when Mundo had taken off by himself: there were just too many reasons why somebody who rode off out here might never ride back. And Mundo was an expert in desert survival compared to Tenchi.

When he came back with the carbine, Mundo was more or less sitting. His face was covered with sweat. He looked ready to keel over.

He glared at Riley. "It's not going to work."

"It has to work."

"Why, because you said so?"

"No," Riley said truthfully. "Because if it doesn't work, we'll both probably die."

After that Mundo said nothing. Riley studied the angle, fussed with the gun. He tried to figure out how to get the maximum leverage without snapping the barrel under the weight of the rock. He tried to figure out how to get close enough to do the job without getting trapped himself.

When at last he was ready, he explained to Mundo exactly what he planned. "You've got to move like a jackrabbit giving tail to a hungry coyote. You can't dawdle a lick. You understand?"

Mundo gazed at him sadly. "I understand you're going to crush me."

"If it's any comfort to you, the stone'll probably crush me, too."

Mundo reached out a pleading hand to Riley. "Do we have to do this? Can't we wait? I know that Julio—"

"Will do his best. So will we. We have to be sure there's still enough of you left to rescue when he gets here."

They sat there, for a moment, just staring at each other without a word. Then Mundo said slowly, "Thanks for trying, Texan."

And Riley said, "It's the least I can do for such a noble Yankee."

The shared a bittersweet smile. Then Riley edged back toward Mundo's knees. He lowered the gun barrel under the edge of the rock and got it in position.

"Count of three," he ordered. "In English."

Mundo leaned forward, hands braced on the ground.

"One," said Riley.

He crouched. "Two."

He leaned closer. "Three!" he shouted, heaving all his weight against the doorway stone.

For just a second, he felt the rock stone lift, felt it fight against the gun. From the corner of his eye, he could see Mundo moving. Fast. As Mundo dragged his body backward, Riley heard the splinter—then the crunch—of wood and metal against rock.

By sundown of the day after she'd left the ruins, Tenchi could clearly see that her horse, still a bit lame from the encounter with the prairie dog hole, was jogging through taller, richer grass. The land was the way Mundo had described his ranch. Maybe—just maybe!—she was finally approaching the Roadrunner.

She'd had plenty of time to think about what she would say when she finally reached the main house. This was no time to mention that she had been intended as Mundo's sister's slave. It was no time to explain about the outlaws, or the stolen horse herd, or the Texan who sat guarding Mundo. All that could wait.

Her only goal right now was to get help for Mundo.

In her mind, she could still see him buried beneath all those rocks. It was hard to believe there was much that even Riley could do to help him. By now he was probably out of danger, fully rescued, or close to death. Either way, the boys still needed help. Somehow she had to convince Julio Rivera that a starving, exhausted Navajo girl in torn and filthy clothes could take him to his aristocratic brother.

Way too soon she got her chance. Seven mounted cowboys abruptly floated up out of the long prairie grass. They wore bandanas over their mouths, maybe to protect them from the dusty wind, but maybe because they didn't want anyone to recognize them.

Tenchi wanted to tell Toland's horse to *run.*

She never got the chance. The men surrounded her with the suddenness of a Navajo thundershower. One of them galloped up behind her and, without even slowing down, lifted her revolver from its holster.

Tenchi held up her hands to be sure nobody shot

her, thinking she might have another gun. She hoped they wouldn't search her knee-high moccasins.

"Navajos sending their womenfolk to do their stealing now?" one cowboy asked in Spanish.

Another said, "Doesn't look quite like any Navajo I ever saw before."

Before they could continue, Tenchi burst out, "I'm here for Mundo. Mundo Rivera. I must tell his brother Julio he is in trouble."

The men gazed nervously at each other.

"Who sent you with this, uh, information?" one asked.

"I came on my own. Mundo is badly injured. I saw it happen."

They stared at her with disbelieving eyes.

"It is true! He is trapped in an old Indian ruin over a day from here." She pointed southeast, the way she'd come.

"How is it you happen to know *Señor* Mundo?" another cowboy asked.

It was too hard to explain. Tenchi just said simply, "He is my friend."

Chapter Twenty-Four

A half hour later, Tenchi found herself in front of a massive adobe house—it looked more like a fort—closed off by wagon-wide gates, tall and sturdy. *"Bienvenidos al rancho del correcaminos,"* said a carved wooden sign. *Correcaminos* was the Spanish word for "roadrunner." She closed her eyes in relief.

The cowboys kept close to Tenchi. One of the men rode ahead, calling out a warning. At once half a dozen muskets appeared from the tops of the walls.

"We need to speak to *El Patrón!*" yelled the cowboy.

"He is busy now."

"Get him anyway! This Navajo girl says she has word of *Señor* Mundo."

There was a shocked silence. "A Navajo? The kidnappers sent a Navajo this time?"

"She says she is on her own. That *Señor* Mundo has been injured. She did not ask for money."

"Money!" Tenchi burst out. "He's dying! An earthquake brought an ancient stone wall down on him. If you won't send somebody to help him, take me to somebody who will!"

Suddenly, a big man, dressed in a finely woven ranch coat and woolen trousers, strutted out to the front of the compound. He carried a rifle. "You watch your mouth, girl," he greeted her coldly. "Nobody here has any reason to listen to a Navajo."

Four other men marched behind him. One of them silently pointed to the horse Tenchi rode. *El Patrón* bent down to check the brand. Tenchi suddenly remembered Mundo doing the same thing when he had first caught up with Toland's horse. Surely it was stolen! But from whom? If Mundo recognized the brand, surely *El Patrón* would, too.

Tenchi struggled to remain calm. *This is the man who will control my life,* she thought bitterly. She knew he was not the sort of man to let a slave escape.

"Tell me what you told the men."

She dared not look at him. "Mundo was camping at an old Indian ruin in the desert when an earthquake hit and a stone wall fell down on him. There's another boy with him, but he's injured, too, and I don't know if he can pull off the huge rocks. Even if he does, they both still need food and water and medicine."

Suddenly she felt the tip of *El Patrón's* rifle beneath her chin. "Tell me who sent you here with all these lies."

"No one." She trembled. "Mundo needs his brother."

"You are riding a horse that belongs to me. I stable no stock to the east, toward what you call this 'ruin.'"

My horses can be found in only three places: on my ranch, with the Yankee troops, and right here, where I am visiting."

"They can also be found on their way to the Staked Plains," she told him boldly. "You can probably find many others with the outlaws who stole this horse."

He jammed the rifle up tighter. "So how is it that *you* are riding one?"

Tenchi knew that if she told him the whole story, he would think she had made it up. Or he would assume that she had, in some way, helped the outlaws who'd stolen his horses and killed his men. She knew *El Patrón* was hard, that he saw Navajos only as non-people. So had Mundo until just yesterday. She hoped his brother would not feel the same.

"I must speak to *Señor* Julio."

"He is not here, and he is not a fool. He would not listen to you anyway. You will tell me the truth or I will shoot you here and now."

Tenchi closed her eyes. What could she tell him? The truth was unbelievable. She wasn't sure she believed it herself.

"Let me see Mundo's sister, then," she begged in desperation. "His sister will send someone to help him."

"I am in charge while the Rivera men are absent. I give you one more chance—"

"No, *señor*, I beg your pardon," a determined female voice suddenly interrupted.

Tenchi's head snapped up. She was looking at a girl about her age, dressed in an embroidered top and green skirt that was adorned with three thick sets of bottom ruffles. The sight of her elegant clothes made Tenchi feel twice as shabby.

"This is Rivera land, and while there is still a Rivera living," the fancy girl declared, "the Riveras will make decisions regarding this family."

The big man did not move his rifle. "You are a child! You have no business—"

"I am old enough to marry your son!" the Hispanic girl snapped at him with a haughtiness that reminded Tenchi of Mundo. "And I am old enough to do whatever it takes to save my brother!"

There was a quiet shift among the cowboys. Some lowered their guns. A few others, it seemed to Tenchi, pointed them ever so subtly at *El Patrón.*

Angrily he challenged, "I just don't want any more trouble to touch your family. When your father left me in charge—"

"He did not leave you in charge. He left my brother, Julio. You stayed because you were afraid to face the Texans!"

Tenchi felt a ghost of hope deep in her heart. This had to be Chayito! No wonder Mundo loved her. He'd been right when he'd said she could deal with *El Patrón!* If Tenchi had to weave for somebody, it might as well be this girl.

"Young lady, you will not speak to me in that fashion! As long as you are married to my son, you will—"

"But I am not married to your son, not yet. I live under my father's roof, and my father would do anything—including shoot you dead—to find a way to rescue his son."

There was a dark, terrible silence. Tenchi dared not breathe. One cowboy cocked his pistol, but no one else moved.

Then *El Patrón* said, "Do as you wish, *señorita*. But this is a hoax, just like the other one. Those Texas bandits convinced your brother to ride to Santa Fe to get the ransom, and now they have sent this girl with some other trick. They probably want to pull me and the rest of the men away so they can take the rest of your father's stock, and mine as well! He would not want me to leave you alone and unprotected, for no reason."

For a moment, the girl hesitated.

El Patrón pressed on. "Besides, your little brother headed toward Albuquerque with the Yankees, and they have all gone north by now, those that survived." His words slashed the sunbaked silence. "How could Mundo have ended up hiding way out in those ruins unless he deserted?"

Quickly, Chayito shook her head. Even her long black hair trembled with her anger. "I do not know how he got there. I do not even know if he is alive. But I do know that if there is the slightest chance that this Navajo is telling the truth, *I will ride to help my brother.*" Before *El Patrón* could speak again, she rushed on. "If tragedy hit your family, I know you'd do the same."

Chapter Twenty-Five

"There!" hollered Tenchi late the next day as the ruins came into view. "That's where I left them!"

Chayito put heels to her horse without a word. She had said little since she'd ordered a man to saddle her best horse and a fine black mare that *Papá* had recently given Mundo. It heartened Tenchi that Mundo's sister brought a mount for him.

She must be expecting to find him alive.

A dozen Roadrunner cowboys, and some who worked for *El Patrón*, rode with them. *El Patrón* had given commands of his own before they'd left the ranch, commands regarding the rescue of all the stock that was still held by the rustlers. But Chayito insisted that nobody was to worry about horses until her brother was safely rescued, and the Roadrunner cowboys paid close attention to Mundo's sister.

They were trailed by a wagon full of food, water, and medical supplies. Chayito had refused to wait for it.

It was obvious that nothing on the face of the earth would keep her from reaching her brother.

As they galloped toward the ruins, Tenchi heard a shout from the butte where she and Mundo had hidden Toland. A man stood on the top, wildly waving his arms.

"Who's that?" Chayito asked. "The Texan?"

Tenchi nodded. She'd told Chayito everything during their long, rough journey. At least everything about Mundo's troubles. She had not mentioned that she had been sold to *El Patrón* for Chayito's wedding.

Chayito called to the men as they drew their guns. "Hold your fire! The man on the butte is my brother's friend!"

One of the cowboys warned her, "No, *señorita*, it is a trap! Look! He is wearing gray Confederate trousers!"

"It's all right!" Chayito ordered. "I'll explain it to you later." Then she leaped off her horse and threw the reins to him.

She ran up the rocky path with Tenchi right behind her. Riley, with one hand on his blood-caked side, came rushing down to greet them.

"Your brother's all right!" he called out to Chayito. "He's battered from bow to stern, but he's gonna make it."

Chayito bowed her head for just a moment and crossed herself. Then she ran by Riley without a word. She threw herself on the ground next to Mundo. He looked terrible. His skin was a mass of bruises—yellow, purple, and brown. Still, Tenchi saw his eyes fill up when he spotted his sister. He tried to smile. Chayito took his hand with both of hers. She pressed it against her face and started crying.

In that instant, Tenchi felt the pain of all she'd missed for so many years. Was this what it was like to be reunited with a family member? Was this how her cousins had last greeted her? Was there anybody here—anybody on earth—who even knew that *she* had been kidnapped and lost in the wilderness also? Anybody who cared that she'd survived?

Then she looked up and saw Riley. He looked so straight and strong that she could have mistaken him for a stranger.

"So you made it, Tenchi," he drawled. "I'm proud of you."

Tenchi was proud of herself, too. Her journey had tested her courage to the limit, but she'd done what she set out to do.

She smiled at Riley. He'd done a fine job himself.

"I don't got words to thank you for all you done for me," he said warmly, "but I'm glad I got a chance to say goodbye."

Tenchi straightened. "You're leaving?"

He glanced toward Chayito, still hovering on the ground near her brother. "Ain't got no choice, now that ya'll are safe and I'm fit to travel. I don't wanna be no prisoner of no Yankees—" his mouth grew taut "—and I won't be no traitor."

Mundo slept well that night. He was exhausted and most of his body was too sore to move, but he had no broken bones or permanent injuries. He managed to eat what the Roadrunner cook had specially prepared for him. He even got to sleep on a soft bed Chayito had ordered to be placed in the canvas-covered wagon. She'd also made sure that Tenchi was fed well and Riley got all the medical care the ranch could offer.

When he woke up in the morning, Riley was crunched inside the wagon.

"Hey, Yankee," he bantered, "you doin' all right?"

Mundo managed to nod. "I guess we're finally even."

"More or less."

They were silent for a moment. There was so much more they could have said, but Mundo realized that it didn't need saying. True friends shared many things without words.

"You getting everything you need?" he finally asked. "If there's anything you want, just ask Chayito—"

"No, she's done enough. There is something else I want from you, though, before I say goodbye."

His words took Mundo off guard. Had he been asleep in the wagon for more than a night? Unconscious for days?

"Goodbye?" he repeated. "Surely you're going to take some time to heal up at the ranch?"

Riley cast a glance through the open end of the wagon. Early morning sunbeams were streaking the pure blue sky. The wind had finally stopped blowing.

"Can't do it, Mundo. Rules are different when lives are at stake. But all that's over now. I gotta get back to my unit."

Mundo felt a flash of anger. "You could stay with us! The war's left us short on help. You could become a Roadrunner cowboy!"

Riley shook his head. "I ain't cut out to be no cowboy. I ain't even cut out to be no fisherman. I'm a soldier, a Texas soldier, as long as this trouble lasts."

His serious blue eyes met Mundo's.

Abruptly Mundo remembered how they'd met. That was the real Riley. If he hadn't been shot, Mundo would never have been anything to him but another captured prisoner. It was only an accident that they'd ended up as friends.

Mundo bit his lip. He couldn't look at Riley.

"The buckskin's broke down. I need another horse."

"You don't need my help for that! You Texans have been stealing our horses since before the Yankees came."

"I don't want to steal one. I want a gift."

"What's the difference? You want to be a Texas soldier. Texas soldiers take what they want! They don't care that we're people, that we have a right to our own land and livestock!"

Riley's lips tightened. "I know it's not fair that your people got stuck in the middle of this. I didn't know that before we came up the Rio Grande, but I understand it now."

"So go back! Or stay here and be one of us," Mundo pleaded.

"I can't. Maybe this ain't the best place for a Texas soldier to be right now, but until we whup the Yankees *everywhere*, Texas needs every man."

Mundo didn't answer.

"I'm a lot better than I was, but I'd still rather not cross the desert without a horse."

"So take a horse! Steal any mount you want."

Riley stood up slowly. He looked long and lanky in the wagon, taller than he'd seemed before. The top of his sandy-colored head even brushed the canvas. "You got a lot to learn yet about real Texans," he drawled darkly. "I'd forage anything from my enemy to keep my country's freedom, Mundo. But ain't no way I'd never steal nothin' from a friend."

Chapter Twenty-Six

Riley dragged his feet a mile or two through sagebrush-speckled sand before he heard hoofbeats pounding after him. He turned and spied Chayito, her pretty face glowing in the morning sun. She was riding a big white horse and leading a fine black one. It was loaded down with overstuffed saddlebags.

"We can't give you guns or ammunition," she announced when she reached him, "but this should keep your stomach full."

With reluctance and relief, Riley took the lead. His carbine had been shattered by the rock, but he figured he could pick up another one on some abandoned battlefield.

"Did your brother say I could take this mare?" he asked Chayito. "Or was it your idea?"

"He wanted you to have it."

"Nobody can say I stole it? I won't be no horsethief."

"It's Mundo's horse. I brought it for him to ride back to the ranch. Nobody but Mundo has any say about what happens to it."

Riley nodded slowly. He was finding it hard to speak.

"What's he gonna ride back to the Roadrunner?"

"He'll ride in the wagon. He's still in a lot of pain."

"I did my best, miss," he apologized. And he had. He'd stretched himself to the breaking point, badly straining some muscles and briefly reopening his wound. But Riley had no complaints. His soreness was a small price to pay for keeping that massive doorway stone from completely crushing Mundo.

"You saved my brother's life. You have nothing to be sorry for."

Chayito leaned down and kissed his barely bearded cheek. One fold of her soft green skirt brushed his Rebel jacket. Riley was glad that, dirty as it was, the jacket no longer dripped fresh blood. He would have been embarrassed to soil Mundo's sister's clothes. Even after two long days and nights in the desert, she still looked like a lady.

"I think this is the first time in my life I've ever had a reason to thank a Texan." Chayito smiled at him brightly. "Don't worry about your buckskin. We'll nurse it back to health."

Riley smiled back.

As she galloped off toward her brother, he mounted Mundo's horse and headed in the opposite direction.

~~~

Tenchi was finishing up a hot, fresh tortilla when Chayito rode back into the camp, dismounted, and tossed her reins to one of the men. She looked tired, but happy. She walked, Tenchi noticed uncomfortably, with the confidence of one born to privilege and wealth.

Instinctively, Tenchi stood up as Chayito approached the fire. A day or two of freedom was not enough to undo half a lifetime's training as a slave.

Chayito smiled at her. "I caught up with Riley. He should do fine with food and a fresh horse."

Tenchi nodded in acknowledgment and unspoken gratitude for her friend. She knew that it had been a hard parting between Riley and Mundo. She'd heard some of it from outside the wagon while she'd been waiting to go in.

"I stayed with your brother until he fell asleep again," she reported. It was what Chayito had ordered her to do. "Is there anything else you need?"

Chayito looked surprised. "I was going to ask you that question."

Tenchi lowered her eyes. "I have no yarn or loom here. I can start weaving as soon as we return to the ranch."

She could not hide the resentment in her voice. How had she let this happen? She'd chosen friendship over freedom, and she did not regret it. But now she had to pay the price.

Chayito took a few steps closer, then settled down on an old log the cowboys had dragged up beside the fire. "Please sit down," she told Tenchi.

Tenchi did. She bit back her anger and tried to remind herself that she was not just speaking to her new owner. *This* was Mundo's sister. Surely it would be better than it had been before.

"This is the first time the Riveras have ever had reason to be indebted to a Navajo," Chayito began slowly. "But you have saved my brother's life. There are not enough words to thank you for what you have done."

Tenchi risked meeting her eyes.

"Mundo has told me . . . how you came to be captured on your way to the Roadrunner. And he has told me that he wants me to give you anything you ask for."

Some of Tenchi's resentment faded. Even in his terrible condition, Mundo had not forgotten her. His sister was strong and kind. Maybe life as Chayito's slave would not be too terrible.

"I had to deal with Riley first because he insisted on leaving right away. Your situation seems a little more complicated, but I promise you, I will find a way to carry out my brother's wishes."

Tenchi's chin jerked up. What did that mean? Did Mundo think she wanted a new skirt to replace her rags? A choice of food? A tiny room that was hers alone instead of a corner of his barn? He'd certainly made it clear he didn't think she was strong enough to return to the Navajos.

"Tenchi," said Chayito slowly, "by law you belong to *El Patrón*. If I marry his son, you will belong to me. I can promise you a decent life, a fair life, maybe the best kind a Navajo can have in New Mexico these days."

Tenchi knew she should have said "thank you." But how could she thank someone for guaranteeing her a life in captivity?

"But my brother says that … you may want to return to your people, even though you've been gone a long time. He doesn't think it's a good idea."

Tenchi's teeth clenched.

"But he also said the choice should be yours to make."

"*Señorita?*" she asked in disbelief. Surely she wasn't saying—

"If you become my property, I will legally free you, if that's what you want, when I complete my wedding ceremony after *Papá* and *Don* Victor come back from battle. And if … I can no longer marry *Don* Victor—" she did not say what might stop the marriage "—then my *papá* will convince *El Patrón* to sell you to us, so we can let you go." She smiled at Tenchi. "After all, *Papá* is a hero. *El Patrón* cannot refuse him. While *El Patrón* stayed back with the women, *Papá* bravely rode off to war."

Tenchi could not believe what she was hearing. Mundo had told Chayito to free her! She was vowing to do it!

But her joy stopped short as she realized that all of Chayito's plans hinged, one way or another, on her father's return from battle. And Tenchi knew all too well that Mundo was not at all sure his father was still alive.

How could Chayito and Mundo free her if the Texans had killed their *papá?*

~~~

El Patrón left the Roadrunner the day after Mundo arrived in the wagon. Julio came home the same day. He looked unutterably weary as he dragged himself into the bedroom where Mundo, in great pain, still lay in bed. Julio plopped down on an old chair that Chayito had brought in. At first he said nothing. Then he gingerly reached out and pulled Mundo close to him.

Mundo gripped him tightly. Neither one needed to say a word.

Later, Julio asked about *Papá*, and Mundo told him everything. He even confessed that he'd run away from the battle. He was still ashamed, but compared to everything that had happened since, it seemed a small thing.

When he was done, Chayito came in with the news that the Riveras' loyal cowboys, and some of *El Patrón*'s, had just returned with dozens of the stolen horses. They had caught up with the rustlers the day after Chayito had reached Mundo. Most of the outlaws had abandoned the stolen herd and begun to run. A few escaped. Kurtzer shot two of *El Patrón*'s men before he fell under a rush of Roadrunner bullets. Because of what he'd done to Mundo, the cowboys refused to bury him.

Mundo could not pretend he was sorry. He loved sharing the news with Tenchi, but they both wished Riley had been there to hear it, too.

Over the next few weeks, while Mundo was recovering, Chayito was his main nurse, but Tenchi regularly spelled her. The women who were still waiting at the Roadrunner for the return of their men fussed over him. And Julio spent many hours in the chair by his bed. They chatted more in the first few days than they had talked in years. Sometimes they discussed the family's past, and sometimes they worried about the future. Mainly they talked about the great battle going on between the Yankees and all the Rebels, not just the Texans.

Mundo had learned a lot about this strange war since he'd first gone off to prove himself to his father. He'd learned that thousands of people on both sides— living farther away than he could ride in half a year— were engaged in war for lots of different reasons. His own people were fighting the Texans because the Texans had overrun their country. The Texans claimed that, in the South, the Yankees had done the same thing. But here in New Mexico, the Texans were the invaders. It was crazy.

Once he tried to explain Riley's thinking to Julio. At first all Julio heard was that he'd been engaged in war talk with the enemy.

"You're telling me that you made friends with a *Texan*? A *Texan* saved your life?"

Julio sounded just as surprised about Mundo's friendship with Tenchi. "You want me to buy this Navajo from *El Patrón* and *free* her?"

"Only if Chayito cannot marry *Don* Victor. If she does, then she can—"

"We will talk about it later," Julio told him. It was the way Julio solved everything.

But Julio had not solved the mystery of *Papá. Papá*

had charged into battle; no one had seen him fall; no one had seen him since. To everyone outside the family, it seemed obvious that he had been killed by the Texans, or at least captured. Many New Mexican prisoners of war had been exchanged by now for Texans, but *El Patrón*'s important friends could learn nothing about *Papá* . . . or *Don* Victor.

There was nobody Mundo could ask about Riley.

Chapter Twenty-Seven

When Riley had left Chayito, he'd struck out across the desert toward Albuquerque. As the days passed, he'd edged north and west along the base of the mountains looking for the army. He took his time. Both he and the fine black mare he named "Road-runner" were in fair shape when they finally ran into Texas troops near Santa Fe.

"Howdy-doo," an old man in a ratty gray uniform greeted Riley. "You look like you been rode hard an' put up wet."

"Pretty much," admitted Riley, without going into the details. He was still afraid that somebody might think he'd been disloyal to Texas if they knew he'd actually saved a New Mexican soldier. "Any word from home? Or back east where they're fightin'?"

"Lots of news; all of it's old. Come join us by the fire and we'll tell you what we know."

Riley slowly dismounted. His side still hurt when he

moved too fast. Besides, he'd been alone so long it felt odd to talk to somebody besides Mundo's horse.

They casually exchanged names and home counties. The old man was from Abilene. He said he had seven children and thirty-two grandkids, so everybody called him "Grandpa." Riley would have told him he'd never called anybody "Grandpa" before but he didn't want the old guy to pity him.

"What unit you with?" Grandpa asked.

"First Regiment." A touch of pride warmed Riley's drawl.

"That so? I don't think the First done made it up here yet. Leastways, we ain't run into 'em. Then again, our boys is scattered all over the place. Long as we keep fightin' them Yankees, I reckon that's all that counts."

Riley nodded. The campfire was twice as big as the one Mundo had built to warm him in the ruins, but the men around it were strangers. Still, they were Texas soldiers. The kind that *hadn't* deserted when things got rough.

"We're with the Third," one of the younger soldiers said. With a thin face and a full beard, he looked tired and friendly as he stood and shook hands with Riley. "Until the First catches up, I don't reckon the captain would mind much if you fell in with us."

"Thanks."

"Got some beans here," said another. "You're welcome to have some. Sorry, it's not much."

Riley hesitated for a moment, remembering how much of the trip up from Texas he and Joey had spent hungry. He didn't want to take what little these kind soldiers had, but it would be rude to refuse to eat with them. It would be worse yet to let them go hungry when he still had food of his own.

"I picked up some good grub from a ranch," he offered.

Grandpa smiled. His two messmates pressed close while Riley divvied up what remained in his saddlebags. A fourth man, no older than Riley, joined them later with fresh information that was being passed from fire to fire. A lieutenant from another unit had seized a letter from a Yankee prisoner with month-old news from Tennessee. Fort Donelson had fallen to the Yankees. Two thousand Rebel troops were reported dead or injured, and twelve thousand had surrendered to General Grant.

The news made Riley sick inside, but more glad than ever that he'd chosen the right path. Mundo didn't understand, but it was very clear to Riley. Texas needed him, and he needed Texas. It was as simple as that.

After supper, the men seemed eager to swap battle stories with Riley. They seemed disappointed that he didn't have much to say.

"Right now, I really ought to see a doctor, if ya'll got one nearby," he explained.

The old man, munching on a now-stale tortilla, pointed him in the right direction. "He ain't much, but he's all we've got."

Neither he nor the other men asked Riley why he needed a doctor, though the bearded one's tired eyes showed curiosity. Grandpa promised to grain the black mare and find Riley a weapon while he visited the hospital tent.

"You're one lucky boy," declared the doctor after he saw the wound and heard Riley's story. "This should have killed you. Should have been stitched, too. Too late to do that now. It's lumping up, healing itself. Going to leave a wicked scar, but I don't see any infection."

He gave Riley some ointment and told him to keep the wound clean. He didn't clarify how that was possible for a soldier on the march in a country that didn't even have enough water to wet the tongues of its lizards.

"Thanks, Doc," Riley said, uncomfortably aware that other injured men were waiting. Still, he had a question he had to ask, and this doctor was the first person he'd seen who might know the answer. "You, uh, ever treat any prisoners?"

"Yankees? Sure."

"I'm looking for a New Mexican. Rich rancher lives a good piece south of here. About your age, I guess. Name's Rivera."

The doctor thought a minute. "No, can't say as I've heard of him. Course he might get a doctor of his own if he's really wealthy."

"Oh yeah, he's wealthy." Riley chuckled bitterly. "He's filthy rich."

"Then I'd try a local doctor. There are a few left in Santa Fe. If you—"

"He wouldn't be with our troops unless they brought him along to exchange. He was in battle down near Albuquerque."

The doctor shook his head. "We traded most of the prisoners before we left." He cocked his head, carefully studied Riley. "Why you looking for this guy? He owe you some money?"

Riley shook his head.

"He shoot you?"

"No."

"You shoot *him?*"

"Nope."

Before the doctor could press him further, Riley lifted the tent flap and headed back to the campfire. He wasn't sure he could justify his concern over a volunteer New Mexican fighting for the Yankees. It would be harder yet—impossible, the way he'd left things with Mundo—to explain that he was bound and determined to find out if any Texan troops still held the missing father of his friend.

Chapter Twenty-Eight

Nearly a month after his first attempted battle, Mundo set off to war again. This time he rode with Julio. Chayito begged them not to go, but New Mexico was running out of time. So were the Riveras. The Texans had stripped clean everything they'd touched from the moment they'd crossed the border. The Roadrunner would be swallowed whole if they were allowed to keep marching.

Mundo had heard that Yankee troops were pressing in from the other side of Santa Fe, heavily enforced with volunteer miners from Colorado. He was bothered that New Mexico could not field enough men of her own to stop the Texans, but his pride was overpowered by his hunger for his country's freedom. He was willing to ride with anybody who was willing to fight the Rebels.

A long line of Roadrunner cowboys trailed the Rivera brothers as they crossed twenty miles of sparse grasslands, then headed up into the mountains. It had rained lightly about a week before, and the dusty winds had somewhat eased. Everywhere Mundo saw signs of spring.

Bright golden poppies sprang up through the sandy soil. Tiny buds sprouted on ocotillos. A roadrunner's nest poked out beneath a strawberry hedgehog cactus. The cactus itself sported bright red and purple blooms.

How can flowers blossom in all this blood? Mundo asked himself as they rushed to join the Yankee regulars. *How can boys stay friends when their people are fighting against each other? How can I go on without knowing what happened to my papá?*

It took two days to urge the horses through heavy brush and deep ravines, but finally one of the men riding up ahead galloped back with news that he had seen a massive group of Yankee troops. The Riveras pressed on and joined them that night. Julio could have reported his volunteers to the commanding officer by himself, but he glanced at Mundo and simply asked, "Shall we go?"

Mundo felt pride burn brightly deep inside, but he said nothing as he reined his mount along beside his brother's. It took them half an hour to find the right tent, and they waited another hour for the officer to return.

"We're New Mexican volunteers, sir," said Julio after they had been introduced.

"First time at war?" he asked, glancing at Mundo.

"No, sir. I've been fighting the Texans a good deal

of my life, and my brother fought recently down near Albuquerque."

Mundo didn't want to think about that battle. He tried to forget how he'd run, how he'd lost his father, how he'd locked horns with an enemy soldier who'd become his friend.

"Then you know what we're up against."

"Yes, sir," said Mundo, since the Yankee was looking at him. "We brought most of our cowboys, too. We're from the Roadrunner Ranch, and—"

"The Roadrunner? I should have realized that when I heard the name 'Rivera.' A small group from your ranch just joined us the other day."

Mundo's heart thudded so hard it hurt. "Our cowboys, sir? Our *papá* is—"

"About a mile from here," the officer replied with a grin. "He's not up to fighting, but your cowboys will only take orders from him."

Julio and Mundo didn't speak as they eagerly spurred their tired horses after the private who'd been ordered to lead them to their father. Julio rode stiffly, his back erect and his head held high. Mundo did likewise, but his heart was scrambling with hope and joy.

"It's just beyond those trees, sir," the private said to Julio. "If you—"

"Thanks!" called Julio as he kicked his horse into a dead run.

Mundo grinned. If Julio could toss pride aside, so could he!

The Rivera brothers galloped into the camp just as the cowboys were making supper. One of them looked up and cried out, *"Señor! Ya vienen sus muchachos!"* Your boys are here!"

Mundo and Julio exchanged a quick glance. *Papá* really was alive!

A moment later they spotted *Don* Victor, rushing toward them with a broad smile. "Mundo! You made it! We were so worried when you disappeared!" Then he asked, "Julio, how is Chayito?"

But *Papá* came rumbling out of the tent before Julio or Mundo could answer.

He looked older, a thousand years older than he'd looked a month before. His gait was slow and awkward, and one bandaged-wrapped arm hung limply by his side. Pleasure filled his eyes as he spotted Julio. But when he realized that Mundo was with his brother, his expression changed to incredible joy and relief.

"Mijo!" he cried. "The Texans did not get you!"

He stumbled forward, eyes red-rimmed and wet, as Mundo swung out of the saddle and ran to him. *Papá* wrapped his good arm around his younger son and held him close, desperately close.

"Forgive me, *mijo*," he whispered. "I have lost so much. I was crazy to put revenge before holding on to what I still have. I can't believe God has granted me another chance with my daughter and my sons."

He let Mundo go only long enough to hug Julio. "You are well?"

"We are fine, *Papá*," Julio assured him. "We were just so worried about you. *El Patrón* could not find out anything about you, and so much has happened that—"

"What has happened?" *Papá* cried out. "Have the Texans reached the ranch? My Chayito—"

"Chayito is well, *Papá,* and the Roadrunner is still safe," Mundo assured him. "But we have much to tell you. After the battle it took me—" he chose his words with care "—a long time to get back home."

Don Victor joined the Riveras for supper and politely asked again for someone to tell him about Chayito. Mundo told him that his sister was well, but at this point she probably thought he was dead. It was obvious to all of them that *Don* Victor was eager to return to his future bride.

Papá wanted to hear everything that had happened to his family since he'd lost track of Mundo in battle. Mundo told him the truth, but it was hard to watch the guilt and sorrow on his *papá*'s face. He kept patting Mundo's arm and moaning softly as he heard everything his younger son had endured. Once he said softly, "You have been through so much, *mijo.* You do not seem the same."

Papá was astonished that Mundo had survived with the help of a Navajo, let alone that he now considered her a friend. But Mundo pressed on, explaining how Tenchi came to be captured, and made it clear to *Papá* and *Don* Victor that one way or another, he would not let them rest until they found a way to free her. He could tell that they did not understand, but after all he'd been through, they were both eager to do anything to make him happy.

Mundo did not go into detail about Riley. When the war was over, he would tell *Papá* that Riley was a Texan ... and his friend. Right now all he had to know was that a young white soldier had saved his son's life.

Mundo did not want to think about Riley anyway. He could only do his duty in the coming battle if he summoned up all his hatred for the Texans and pushed away the memory of his Texan friend.

In the morning, Mundo left the tent while everyone was still sleeping. He had his horse half-saddled when Julio and *Papá* joined him. Mundo was afraid his *papá* would forbid him to go into battle. He didn't want to show disrespect—especially now—but he knew that he could never let anyone treat him like a boy again.

Papá stared at his younger son for some time before he spoke. "You will be careful?" he asked slowly.

Mundo swallowed hard. "Yes, *Papá.*"

"You will watch out for your brother?" he asked Julio.

Julio nodded. "And he will watch out for me."

Papa hugged them both. Julio swung into the saddle. Mundo leaped up on his own horse.

Then, for the first time ever, his *papá* shook his hand.

They rode for several hours before some Yankee regulars up ahead stumbled over Texas troops. Instantly Mundo's unit dismounted and engaged the enemy, rushing on foot over the rocks and jagged hills.

This time, it did not occur to him to run. He was afraid, but he was fighting for his country, for his land, for his family. He would stand his ground.

Mundo loaded his single-shot musket. He aimed and fired.

All around him, bullets started pinging, men shouted and cried out. Some of them were hit and crumpled to the ground.

Still, inch by inch, the line pressed forward. Past old dead stumps and mighty oaks, past ponderosa and Apache pines. Everywhere they marched, more Texans met them. The canyons echoed with the sharp sound of booming guns.

It didn't take long before the Roadrunner volunteers got separated in the rough terrain of the Sangre de Cristo Mountains. *Don* Victor disappeared with a group of cowboys and Yankee soldiers, but Julio stayed close to Mundo.

For hours, the Rivera brothers fought together in the warm spring sun. Mundo loaded and fired and dodged and rolled, over and over and over again, until he had no more strength to crawl over boulders, no more strength to watch men die. He barely had strength to hold up his musket.

And then, without warning, he found himself half-sliding into a new ravine, deep and narrow. A dozen Texans were shooting from the other side.

One of them fired at Mundo. Julio fired back. Mundo took aim, fired, and desperately tried to reload.

Above the roar of battle, he glanced across the ravine.

Half-hidden by a stand of ponderosas, there stood a tall, skinny Texan boy a few years older than Mundo. His eyes were blue, and his sandy hair was dirty. His Confederate jacket was half-open, ripped up, blood-stained. He thrust the muzzle of a beat-up carbine toward the Riveras.

It was Riley.

Mundo stopped. He couldn't seem to move his fingers, couldn't load his gun.

He couldn't believe that Riley would shoot him.

But Julio didn't know that there was anything special about the Texan who was aiming at his little brother. Mundo wanted to cry out, to beg Julio not to shoot Riley, to beg Riley not to shoot *him*. But no words came out of his mouth. He was frozen.

Riley seemed to be frozen, too. For just a moment he lowered his carbine and stared across the sumac-choked ravine into Mundo's anguished eyes.

Then another nearby Texan started shooting in Mundo's direction. A bullet whizzed by his chin. Julio fired back. At once the soldier focused on Julio. Edging back toward the ponderosas that shielded Riley, he kept on firing.

Mundo knew he had to lift his musket. His brother needed him.

But how could he shoot a soldier who crouched just inches away from Riley? Mundo's aim wasn't that good. He couldn't just move his musket an inch one way or the other and be sure to hit his target! The chances were fifty-fifty that he would hit his friend.

But if he didn't shoot, the other soldier might shoot his brother.

So might Riley.

Suddenly Riley yelled, "I think you got one! I'll get the other!" Then he swung his carbine back at Mundo.

It took Mundo only a moment to read Riley's mind. He was going to trick the other soldiers into shooting in some other direction! He would only pretend to kill Mundo.

To Julio he shouted in Spanish, "Don't shoot! Don't shoot! Don't shoot!"

The glare Julio flashed at Mundo left no doubt that he thought his little brother had lost his mind. Then he took deliberate aim at Riley.

Mundo coiled up like a striking rattler and threw himself at Julio. "Don't shoot!" he screamed again as both of them tumbled down the rocky slope. The rifle clattered along with them.

Julio cuffed him aside like a mother bear might bat her cub. Unarmed, he threw himself back in front of his little brother, boldly facing the firing Texans. He tried to keep covering Mundo while he crawled forward for his gun.

But it had skidded several feet down the bluff. Mundo knew that long before his brother reached the rifle, he'd be ripped apart by enemy bullets.

Without thinking of himself, Mundo leaped to his feet. "Riley!" he screamed, wildly waving both hands. "Stop! He's my brother!"

Riley didn't blink an eye. He moved the barrel of his carbine until it was pointed at Julio, still crawling toward his gun. He fired once. Julio's rifle exploded. Then Riley lifted the barrel and turned once more toward Mundo.

As Mundo stood there in disbelief, Riley aimed straight at him and fired his carbine ... again and again and again.

Epilogue

Throughout April, the families who'd come to the wedding drifted back to their ranches, and the cowboys showed up one by one. The Riveras were among the last to return. They'd chased the Texans clear down the Rio Grande and fought to the bitter end.

It was a beautiful afternoon in early May when the Roadrunner welcomed home its men. Four weary horses plodded toward the blooming paloverdes that graced the main gates. Mundo and Julio rode in front, with their *papá* and *Don* Victor right behind them.

Chayito tugged her skirt clear up above her ankles to run through the long grama grass, racing first to greet her father. Tenchi watched as he clambered off the horse, oblivious of one arm that was tightly wrapped in a sling. He wrapped his good arm around his daughter and fiercely held her close.

They both cried.

Tenchi heard him murmur, "We finally drove them from our country. May your mother's soul rest in peace. Maybe *my* soul can find peace at last."

Tenchi had never seen *Don* Victor before, but one glance told her he was not like his father. He did not sit a horse with arrogance like *El Patrón*, but with the humble pride of a man who has just finished a job well done. He swung out of the saddle, waited until Chayito released her *papá*, then bowed graciously and kissed her hand. She favored him with a welcoming smile before she turned to greet her brothers.

Julio looked as strong as ever, but Mundo looked different to Tenchi, so much older and worn. She dared not put her arms around him the way Chayito did. She was still a captive servant—for just a little while longer!—and did not have the rights of a relative, even though Chayito always insisted that she dine with the family.

Later that night, after a celebrational supper, Mundo asked Tenchi to take a walk with him.

At first, he said nothing. He did not even look at her. His black eyes joyfully drank in his beloved ranch— every clump of needlegrass, every half-empty horsebarn, every clacking hen. The Roadrunner had lost a lot to the Texans this spring, even though the Confederate Army had never reached its gates. The Rivera men had all gone to battle, sent their cowboys, and donated countless supplies and horses. But Tenchi knew that none of the family regretted the sacrifice. The enemy had been banished from New Mexico. They could all sleep well at night and hold their heads up high again.

Finally Mundo looked at Tenchi. "My family has treated you well in my absence?" he asked.

She nodded. "They've been very kind."

"I have spoken to *Don* Victor at length about your ... situation, Tenchi. He says he will take care of things with *El Patrón*. You are free to leave the Roadrunner at any time."

Tenchi's heart lurched. She had hoped for these words, prayed for them, but she still could hardly believe that her dream had come true. "Any time? You mean ... right now?"

Mundo's expression sobered. "Yes, right now, if that's what you want to do." He took a deep breath. "But there is no hurry. You should plan well and let me gather up the supplies and horses you will need for such a journey. You are welcome to stay here as long as you wish, as a guest." He lightly touched her shoulder. "And as my friend."

How wrong I was about Mundo, Tenchi realized gratefully. *I thought he was a heartless rich kid when I first met him. How much he has changed!*

She remembered that terrible first night when they'd both tried to escape from the rustlers. How certain she'd been that loaning Mundo her knife would kill forever her only chance at freedom! *What would have happened to me,* she wondered, *if Riley hadn't forced me to help the two of them?* There was no way she could ever thank Mundo for what he and his family had done.

Tenchi didn't try to find the right words. She just slipped her arms around Mundo's neck and gave him a thank-you hug. He hugged her back, then let her go.

It was hard for Tenchi to speak. "I need to go back to my people and see . . . how things are, Mundo. After that . . . " She trailed off uncertainly.

"After that you are welcome to return any time. *Mi casa es su casa,*" he said with the warmth the Riveras extended to their equals.

Tenchi fought back tears as she smiled her gratitude. Then she said, "I won't forget you, Mundo. Or your sister. You were so right about her."

Mundo replied solemnly, "We're both lucky to have her. So is *Don* Victor."

The Rivera pride still lingered in his voice, but now it graced his words with manly respect for his family instead of the boyish bravado Tenchi had heard when he'd first mentioned Chayito only two months ago.

He glanced around, as though to be sure they were alone, before he confided, "I saw Riley."

"Where?"

"In battle."

Tenchi's stomach tightened. "Is he all right?"

Mundo nodded. "He tried to shoot me. Half a dozen times. Missed Julio, too. He never even came close."

Tenchi stared at him. "That's not possible, Mundo! Even half-conscious, Riley's a dead-eye shot. He couldn't aim to kill you more than once and miss!"

"I know," he said happily. *"I know!"*

Then his face split into a joyful grin.

ABOUT THE AUTHOR

When Suzanne made a change from teaching elementary to middle school, she became intimately involved with the literature of that age and focused on helping her students develop their love of reading. Her students are a valuable test audience in the development of her books.

Suzanne Pierson Ellison wrote over twenty books for adults before Rising Moon published *The Last Warrior,* her first book for young people. *Best of Enemies* combines her interest in the Civil War, the Southwest, and the equality of all children.

Along with American history, Suzanne's many interests include birdwatching, quilting, music, Native American culture, and the Dodgers. She lives in Ventura, California, with her husband, Scott, teenaged daughter Tara, and four beloved cats.